Nathaniel Hawthorne (July 4, 1804 – May 19, 1864) was an American novelist, dark romantic, and short story writer. His works often focus on history, morality, and religion. He was born in 1804 in Salem, Massachusetts, to Nathaniel Hathorne and the former Elizabeth Clarke Manning. His ancestors include John Hathorne, the only judge involved in the Salem witch trials who never repented of his actions. He entered Bowdoin College in 1821, was elected to Phi Beta Kappa in 1824, and graduated in 1825. He published his first work in 1828, the novel Fanshawe; he later tried to suppress it, feeling that it was not equal to the standard of his later work. He published several short stories in periodicals, which he collected in 1837 as Twice-Told Tales. The next year, he became engaged to Sophia Peabody. He worked at the Boston Custom House and joined Brook Farm, a transcendentalist community, before marrying Peabody in 1842. The couple moved to The Old Manse in Concord, Massachusetts, later moving to Salem, the Berkshires, then to The Wayside in Concord. (Source: Wikipedia)

Literary works:
Fanshawe (published anonymously, 1828)
The New Adam and Eve (1843)
The Scarlet Letter (1850)
The House of the Seven Gables (1851)
The Blithedale Romance (1852)
The Marble Faun: Or, The Romance of Monte Beni (1860)
The Dolliver Romance (1863) (unfinished)
Septimius Felton; or, the Elixir of Life (unfinished)
Doctor Grimshawe's Secret: A Romance (unfinished, 1882)
Twice-Told Tales (1837)
Grandfather's Chair (1840)
Mosses from an Old Manse (1846)
A Wonder-Book for Girls and Boys (1851)
Tanglewood Tales (1853)

SEPTIMIUS FELTON
OR, THE ELIXIR OF
LIFE
NATHANIEL HAWTHORNE

PRINCE CLASSICS

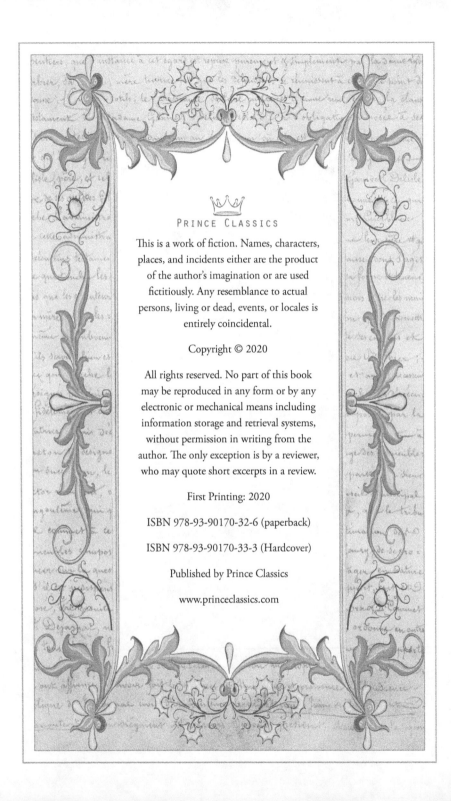

PRINCE CLASSICS

First Printing: 2020

ISBN 978-93-90170-32-6 (paperback)

ISBN 978-93-90170-33-3 (Hardcover)

Published by Prince Classics

www.princeclassics.com

Contents

SEPTIMIUS FELTON
OR, THE ELIXIR OF
LIFE

Introductory Note.

The existence of this story, posthumously published, was not known to any one but Hawthorne himself, until some time after his death, when the manuscript was found among his papers. The preparation and copying of his Note-Books for the press occupied the most of Mrs. Hawthorne's available time during the interval from 1864 to 1870; but in the latter year, having decided to publish the unfinished romance, she began the task of putting together its loose sheets and deciphering the handwriting, which, towards the close of Hawthorne's life, had grown somewhat obscure and uncertain. Her death occurred while she was thus engaged, and the transcription was completed by her daughters. The book was then issued simultaneously in America and England, in 1871.

Although "Septimius Felton" appeared so much later than "The Marble Faun," it was conceived and, in another form, begun before the Italian romance had presented itself to the author's mind. The legend of a bloody foot leaving its imprint where it passed, which figures so prominently in the following fiction, was brought to Hawthorne's notice on a visit to Smithell's Hall, Lancashire, England. [Footnote: See English Note-Books, April 7, and August 25, 1855.] Only five days after hearing of it, he made a note in his journal, referring to "my Romance," which had to do with a plot involving the affairs of a family established both in England and New England; and it seems likely that he had already begun to associate the bloody footstep with this project. What is extraordinary, and must be regarded as an unaccountable coincidence—one of the strange premonitions of genius—is that in 1850, before he had ever been to England and before he knew of the existence of Smithell's Hall, he had jotted down in his Note-Book, written in America, this suggestion: "The print in blood of a naked foot to be traced through the street of a town." The idea of treating in fiction the attempt to renew youth or to attain an earthly immortality had engaged his fancy quite early in his career, as we discover from "Doctor Heidegger's Experiment," in the "Twice-Told Tales." In 1840, also, we find in the journal: "If a man were sure of living forever, he would not care about his offspring." The "Mosses from an Old Manse" supply another link in this train of reflection; for "The Virtuoso's Collection" includes some of the elixir vitae "in an antique sepulchral urn." The narrator there represents himself as refusing to quaff it. "'No; I desire not an earthly immortality,' said I. 'Were man to live longer on earth, the spiritual would die out of him.... There is a celestial something within us that requires, after a certain time, the atmosphere of heaven to preserve it from ruin.'" On the other hand, just before hearing, for the first time, the legend of Smithell's Hall, he wrote in his English journal:–

"God himself cannot compensate us for being born for any period short of eternity. All the misery endured here constitutes a claim for another life, and still more all the happiness; because all true happiness involves something more than the earth owns, and needs something more than a mortal capacity for the enjoyment of it." It is sufficiently clear that he had meditated on the main theme of "Septimius Felton," at intervals, for many years.

When, in August, 1855, Hawthorne went by invitation to Smithell's Hall, the lady of the manor, on his taking leave, asked him "to write a ghost-story for her house;" and he observes in his notes, "the legend is a good one." Three years afterwards, in 1858, on the eve of departure for France and Italy, he began to sketch the outline of a romance laid in England, and having for its hero an American who goes thither to assert his inherited rights in an old manor-house possessing the peculiarity of a supposed bloody foot-print on the threshold-stone. This sketch, which appears in the present edition as "The Ancestral Footstep," was in journal form, the story continuing from day to day, with the dates attached. There remains also the manuscript without elate, recently edited under the title "Dr. Grimshawe's Secret," which bears a resemblance to some particulars in "Septimius Felton."

Nothing further seems to have been done in this direction by the author until he had been to Italy, had written "The Marble Faun," and again returned to The Wayside, his home at Concord. It was then, in 1861, that he took up once more the "Romance of Immortality," as the sub-title of the English edition calls it. "I have not found it possible," he wrote to Mr. Bridge, who remained his confidant, "to occupy my mind with its usual trash and nonsense during these anxious times; but as the autumn advances, I myself sitting down at my desk and blotting successive sheets of paper as of yore." Concerning this place, The Wayside, he had said in a letter to George William Curtis, in 1852: "I know nothing of the history of the house, except Thoreau's telling me that it was inhabited a generation or two ago by a man who believed he should never die." It was this legendary personage whom he now proceeded to revive and embody as Septimius; and the scene of the story was placed at The Wayside itself and the neighboring house, belonging to Mr. Bronson Alcott, both of which stand at the base of a low ridge running beside the Lexington road, in the village of Concord. Rose Garfield is mentioned as living "in a small house, the site of which is still indicated by the cavity of a cellar, in which I this very summer planted some sunflowers." The cellar-site remains at this day distinctly visible near the boundary of the land formerly owned by Hawthorne.

Attention may here perhaps appropriately be called to the fact that some of the ancestors of President Garfield settled at Weston, not many miles from Concord, and that the name is still borne by dwellers in the vicinity. One of the last letters written by the President was an acceptance of an invitation to visit Concord; and it was his intention to journey thither by carriage, incognito, from Boston, passing through the scenes where those ancestors had lived, and entering the village by the old Lexington road, on which The Wayside faces. It is an interesting coincidence that Hawthorne should have chosen for his first heroine's name, either intentionally or through unconscious association, this one which belonged to the region.

The house upon which the story was thus centred, and where it was written, had been a farm-house, bought and for a time occupied by Hawthorne previous to his departure for Europe. On coming back to it, he made some additions to the old wooden structure, and caused to be built a low tower, which rose above the irregular roofs of the older and newer portions, thus supplying him with a study lifted out of reach of noise or interruption, and in a slight degree recalling the tower in which he had taken so much pleasure at the Villa Montauto. The study was extremely simple in its appointments, being finished chiefly in stained wood, with a vaulted plaster ceiling, and containing, besides a few pictures and some plain furniture, a writing-table, and a shelf at which Hawthorne sometimes wrote standing. A story has gone abroad and is widely believed, that, on mounting the steep stairs leading to this study, he passed through a trap-door and afterwards placed upon it the chair in which he sat, so that intrusion or interruption became physically impossible. It is wholly unfounded. There never was any trap-door, and no precaution of the kind described was ever taken. Immediately behind the house the hill rises in artificial terraces, which, during the romancer's residence, were grassy and planted with fruit-trees. He afterwards had evergreens set out there, and directed the planting of other trees, which still attest his preference for thick verdure. The twelve acres running back over the hill were closely covered with light woods, and across the road lay a level tract of eight acres more, which included a garden and orchard. From his study Hawthorne could overlook a good part of his modest domain; the view embraced a stretch of road lined with trees, wide meadows, and the hills across the shallow valley. The branches of trees rose on all sides as if to embower the house, and birds and bees flew about his casement, through which came the fresh perfumes of the woods, in summer.

In this spot "Septimius Felton" was written; but the manuscript, thrown aside, was mentioned in the Dedicatory Preface to "Our Old Home" as an "abortive project." As will be found explained in the Introductory Notes to "The Dolliver Romance" and "The Ancestral Footstep," that phase of the same general design which was developed in the "Dolliver" was intended to take the place of this unfinished sketch, since resuscitated.

G.P.L.

Preface.

The following story is the last written by my father. It is printed as it was found among his manuscripts. I believe it is a striking specimen of the peculiarities and charm of his style, and that it will have an added interest for brother artists, and for those who care to study the method of his composition, from the mere fact of its not having received his final revision. In any case, I feel sure that the retention of the passages within brackets (e. g. p. 253), which show how my father intended to amplify some of the descriptions and develop more fully one or two of the character studies, will not be regretted by appreciative readers. My earnest thanks are due to Mr. Robert Browning for his kind assistance and advice in interpreting the manuscript, otherwise so difficult to me.

UNA HAWTHORNE.

Septimius Felton; Or, The Elixir of Life.

It was a day in early spring; and as that sweet, genial time of year and atmosphere calls out tender greenness from the ground,–beautiful flowers, or leaves that look beautiful because so long unseen under the snow and decay,– so the pleasant air and warmth had called out three young people, who sat on a sunny hill-side enjoying the warm day and one another. For they were all friends: two of them young men, and playmates from boyhood; the third, a girl, who, two or three years younger than themselves, had been the object of their boy-love, their little rustic, childish gallantries, their budding affections; until, growing all towards manhood and womanhood, they had ceased to talk about such matters, perhaps thinking about them the more.

These three young people were neighbors' children, dwelling in houses that stood by the side of the great Lexington road, along a ridgy hill that rose abruptly behind them, its brow covered with a wood, and which stretched, with one or two breaks and interruptions, into the heart of the village of Concord, the county town. It was in the side of this hill that, according to tradition, the first settlers of the village had burrowed in caverns which they had dug out for their shelter, like swallows and woodchucks. As its slope was towards the south, and its ridge and crowning woods defended them from the northern blasts and snow-drifts, it was an admirable situation for the fierce New England winter; and the temperature was milder, by several degrees, along this hill-side than on the unprotected plains, or by the river, or in any other part of Concord. So that here, during the hundred years that had elapsed since the first settlement of the place, dwellings had successively risen close to the hill's foot, and the meadow that lay on the other side of the road–a fertile tract–had been cultivated; and these three young people were the children's children's children of persons of respectability who had dwelt there,–Rose Garfield, in a small house, the site of which is still indicated by the cavity of a cellar, in which I this very past summer planted some sunflowers to thrust their great disks out from the hollow and allure the bee and the humming-bird; Robert Hagburn, in a house of somewhat more pretension, a hundred yards or so nearer to the village, standing back from the road in the broader space which the retreating hill, cloven by a gap in that place, afforded; where some elms intervened between it and the road, offering a site which some person of a natural taste for the gently picturesque had seized upon. Those same elms, or their successors, still flung a noble shade over the same old house, which the magic hand of Alcott has improved by the touch that throws grace, amiableness, and natural beauty over scenes that have little pretension in themselves.

Now, the other young man, Septimius Felton, dwelt in a small wooden house, then, I suppose, of some score of years' standing,—a two-story house, gabled before, but with only two rooms on a floor, crowded upon by the hill behind,—a house of thick walls, as if the projector had that sturdy feeling of permanence in life which incites people to make strong their earthly habitations, as if deluding themselves with the idea that they could still inhabit them; in short, an ordinary dwelling of a well-to-do New England farmer, such as his race had been for two or three generations past, although there were traditions of ancestors who had led lives of thought and study, and possessed all the erudition that the universities of England could bestow. Whether any natural turn for study had descended to Septimius from these worthies, or how his tendencies came to be different from those of his family,—who, within the memory of the neighborhood, had been content to sow and reap the rich field in front of their homestead,—so it was, that Septimius had early manifested a taste for study. By the kind aid of the good minister of the town he had been fitted for college; had passed through Cambridge by means of what little money his father had left him and by his own exertions in school-keeping; and was now a recently decorated baccalaureate, with, as was understood, a purpose to devote himself to the ministry, under the auspices of that reverend and good friend whose support and instruction had already stood him in such stead.

Now here were these young people, on that beautiful spring morning, sitting on the hill-side, a pleasant spectacle of fresh life,—pleasant, as if they had sprouted like green things under the influence of the warm sun. The girl was very pretty, a little freckled, a little tanned, but with a face that glimmered and gleamed with quick and cheerful expressions; a slender form, not very large, with a quick grace in its movements; sunny hair that had a tendency to curl, which she probably favored at such moments as her household occupation left her; a sociable and pleasant child, as both of the young men evidently thought. Robert Hagburn, one might suppose, would have been the most to her taste; a ruddy, burly young fellow, handsome, and free of manner, six feet high, famous through the neighborhood for strength and athletic skill, the early promise of what was to be a man fit for all offices of active rural life, and to be, in mature age, the selectman, the deacon, the representative, the colonel. As for Septimius, let him alone a moment or two, and then they would see him, with his head bent down, brooding, brooding, his eyes fixed on some chip, some stone, some common plant, any commonest thing, as if it were the clew and index to some mystery; and when, by chance startled out of these meditations, he lifted his eyes, there would be a kind of perplexity, a dissatisfied, foiled look in them, as if of his speculations he found no end. Such was now the case, while Robert and the girl were running on with a gay talk about a serious subject, so that, gay as it was, it was interspersed with little thrills of fear on the girl's part, of excitement on Robert's. Their talk was of public trouble.

"My grandfather says," said Rose Garfield, "that we shall never be able to stand against old England, because the men are a weaker race than he remembers in his day,–weaker than his father, who came from England,–and the women slighter still; so that we are dwindling away, grandfather thinks; only a little sprightlier, he says sometimes, looking at me."

"Lighter, to be sure," said Robert Hagburn; "there is the lightness of the Englishwomen compressed into little space. I have seen them and know. And as to the men, Rose, if they have lost one spark of courage and strength that their English forefathers brought from the old land,–lost any one good quality without having made it up by as good or better,–then, for my part, I don't want the breed to exist any longer. And this war, that they say is coming on, will be a good opportunity to test the matter. Septimius! Don't you think so?"

"Think what?" asked Septimius, gravely, lifting up his head.

"Think! why, that your countrymen are worthy to live," said Robert Hagburn, impatiently. "For there is a question on that point."

"It is hardly worth answering or considering," said Septimius, looking at him thoughtfully. "We live so little while, that (always setting aside the effect on a future existence) it is little matter whether we live or no."

"Little matter!" said Rose, at first bewildered, then laughing,—"little matter! when it is such a comfort to live, so pleasant, so sweet!"

"Yes, and so many things to do," said Robert; "to make fields yield produce; to be busy among men, and happy among the women-folk; to play, work, fight, and be active in many ways."

"Yes; but so soon stilled, before your activity has come to any definite end," responded Septimius, gloomily. "I doubt, if it had been left to my choice, whether I should have taken existence on such terms; so much trouble of preparation to live, and then no life at all; a ponderous beginning, and nothing more."

"Do you find fault with Providence, Septimius?" asked Rose, a feeling of solemnity coming over her cheerful and buoyant nature. Then she burst out a-laughing. "How grave he looks, Robert; as if he had lived two or three lives already, and knew all about the value of it. But I think it was worth while to be born, if only for the sake of one such pleasant spring morning as this; and God gives us many and better things when these are past."

"We hope so," said Septimius, who was again looking on the ground. "But who knows?"

"I thought you knew," said Robert Hagburn. "You have been to college, and have learned, no doubt, a great many things. You are a student of theology, too, and have looked into these matters. Who should know, if not you?"

"Rose and you have just as good means of ascertaining these points as I," said Septimius; "all the certainty that can be had lies on the surface, as it should, and equally accessible to every man or woman. If we try to grope deeper, we labor for naught, and get less wise while we try to be more so.

If life were long enough to enable us thoroughly to sift these matters, then, indeed!–but it is so short!"

"Always this same complaint," said Robert. "Septimius, how long do you wish to live?"

"Forever!" said Septimius. "It is none too long for all I wish to know."

"Forever?" exclaimed Rose, shivering doubtfully. "Ah, there would come many, many thoughts, and after a while we should want a little rest."

"Forever?" said Robert Hagburn. "And what would the people do who wish to fill our places? You are unfair, Septimius. Live and let live! Turn about! Give me my seventy years, and let me go,–my seventy years of what this life has,–toil, enjoyment, suffering, struggle, fight, rest,–only let me have my share of what's going, and I shall be content."

"Content with leaving everything at odd ends; content with being nothing, as you were before!"

"No, Septimius, content with heaven at last," said Rose, who had come out of her laughing mood into a sweet seriousness. "Oh dear! think what a worn and ugly thing one of these fresh little blades of grass would seem if it were not to fade and wither in its time, after being green in its time."

"Well, well, my pretty Rose," said Septimius apart, "an immortal weed is not very lovely to think of, that is true; but I should be content with one thing, and that is yourself, if you were immortal, just as you are at seventeen, so fresh, so dewy, so red-lipped, so golden-haired, so gay, so frolicsome, so gentle."

"But I am to grow old, and to be brown and wrinkled, gray-haired and ugly," said Rose, rather sadly, as she thus enumerated the items of her decay, "and then you would think me all lost and gone. But still there might be youth underneath, for one that really loved me to see. Ah, Septimius Felton! such love as would see with ever-new eyes is the true love." And she ran away and left him suddenly, and Robert Hagburn departing at the same time, this little knot of three was dissolved, and Septimius went along the wayside wall, thoughtfully, as was his wont, to his own dwelling. He had stopped for some moments on the threshold, vaguely enjoying, it is probable, the light and warmth of the new spring day and the sweet air, which was somewhat unwonted to the young man, because he was accustomed to spend much of his day in thought and study within doors, and, indeed, like most studious young men, was overfond of the fireside, and of making life as artificial as he could, by fireside heat and lamplight, in order to suit it to the artificial, intellectual, and moral atmosphere which he derived from books, instead of living healthfully in the open air, and among his fellow-beings. Still he felt the pleasure of being warmed through by this natural heat, and, though blinking a little from its superfluity, could not but confess an enjoyment and cheerfulness in this flood of morning light that came aslant the hill-side. While he thus stood, he felt a friendly hand laid upon his shoulder, and, looking up, there was the minister of the village, the old friend of Septimius, to whose advice and aid it was owing that Septimius had followed his instincts by going to college, instead of spending a thwarted and dissatisfied life in the field that fronted the house. He was a man of middle age, or little beyond, of a sagacious, kindly aspect; the experience, the lifelong, intimate acquaintance with many concerns of his people being more apparent in him than the scholarship for which he had been early distinguished. A tanned man, like one who labored in his own grounds occasionally; a man of homely, plain address, which, when occasion called for it, he could readily exchange for the polished manner of one who had seen a more refined world than this about him.

"Well, Septimius," said the minister, kindly, "have you yet come to any conclusion about the subject of which we have been talking?"

"Only so far, sir," replied Septimius, "that I find myself every day less inclined to take up the profession which I have had in view so many years. I do not think myself fit for the sacred desk."

"Surely not; no one is," replied the clergyman; "but if I may trust my own judgment, you have at least many of the intellectual qualifications that should adapt you to it. There is something of the Puritan character in you, Septimius, derived from holy men among your ancestors; as, for instance, a deep, brooding turn, such as befits that heavy brow; a disposition to meditate on things hidden; a turn for meditative inquiry,–all these things, with grace to boot, mark you as the germ of a man who might do God service. Your reputation as a scholar stands high at college. You have not a turn for worldly business."

"Ah, but, sir," said Septimius, casting down his heavy brows, "I lack something within."

"Faith, perhaps," replied the minister; "at least, you think so."

"Cannot I know it?" asked Septimius.

"Scarcely, just now," said his friend. "Study for the ministry; bind your thoughts to it; pray; ask a belief, and you will soon find you have it. Doubts may occasionally press in; and it is so with every clergyman. But your prevailing mood will be faith."

"It has seemed to me," observed Septimius, "that it is not the prevailing mood, the most common one, that is to be trusted. This is habit, formality, the shallow covering which we close over what is real, and seldom suffer to be blown aside. But it is the snake-like doubt that thrusts out its head, which gives us a glimpse of reality. Surely such moments are a hundred times as real as the dull, quiet moments of faith or what you call such."

"I am sorry for you," said the minister; "yet to a youth of your frame of character, of your ability I will say, and your requisition for something profound in the grounds of your belief, it is not unusual to meet this trouble. Men like you have to fight for their faith. They fight in the first place to win it, and ever afterwards to hold it. The Devil tilts with them daily and often seems to win."

"Yes; but," replied Septimius, "he takes deadly weapons now. If he meet me with the cold pure steel of a spiritual argument, I might win or lose, and still not feel that all was lost; but he takes, as it were, a great clod of earth, massive rocks and mud, soil and dirt, and flings it at me overwhelmingly; so that I am buried under it."

"How is that?" said the minister. "Tell me more plainly."

"May it not be possible," asked Septimius, "to have too profound a sense of the marvellous contrivance and adaptation of this material world to require or believe in anything spiritual? How wonderful it is to see it all alive on this spring day, all growing, budding! Do we exhaust it in our little life? Not so; not in a hundred or a thousand lives. The whole race of man, living from the beginning of time, have not, in all their number and multiplicity and in all their duration, come in the least to know the world they live in! And how is this rich world thrown away upon us, because we live in it such a moment! What mortal work has ever been done since the world began! Because we have no time. No lesson is taught. We are snatched away from our study before we have learned the alphabet. As the world now exists, I confess it to you frankly, my dear pastor and instructor, it seems to me all a failure, because we do not live long enough."

"But the lesson is carried on in another state of being!"

"Not the lesson that we begin here," said Septimius. "We might as well train a child in a primeval forest, to teach him how to live in a European court. No, the fall of man, which Scripture tells us of, seems to me to have its operation in this grievous shortening of earthly existence, so that our life here at all is grown ridiculous."

"Well, Septimius," replied the minister, sadly, yet not as one shocked by what he had never heard before, "I must leave you to struggle through this form of unbelief as best you may, knowing that it is by your own efforts that you must come to the other side of this slough. We will talk further another time. You are getting worn out, my young friend, with much study and anxiety. It were well for you to live more, for the present, in this earthly life that you prize so highly. Cannot you interest yourself in the state of this country, in this coming strife, the voice of which now sounds so hoarsely and so near us? Come out of your thoughts and breathe another air."

"I will try," said Septimius.

"Do," said the minister, extending his hand to him, "and in a little time you will find the change."

He shook the young man's hand kindly, and took his leave, while Septimius entered his house, and turning to the right sat down in his study, where, before the fireplace, stood the table with books and papers. On the shelves around the low-studded walls were more books, few in number but of an erudite appearance, many of them having descended to him from learned ancestors, and having been brought to light by himself after long lying in dusty closets; works of good and learned divines, whose wisdom he had happened, by help of the Devil, to turn to mischief, reading them by the light of hell-fire. For, indeed, Septimius had but given the clergyman the merest partial glimpse of his state of mind. He was not a new beginner in doubt; but, on the contrary, it seemed to him as if he had never been other than a doubter and questioner, even in his boyhood; believing nothing, although a thin veil of reverence had kept him from questioning some things. And now the new, strange thought of the sufficiency of the world for man, if man were only sufficient for that, kept recurring to him; and with it came a certain sense, which he had been conscious of before, that he, at least, might never die. The feeling was not peculiar to Septimius. It is an instinct, the meaning of which is mistaken. We have strongly within us the sense of an undying principle, and we transfer that true sense to this life and to the body, instead of interpreting it justly as the promise of spiritual immortality.

So Septimius looked up out of his thoughts, and said proudly: "Why should I die? I cannot die, if worthy to live. What if I should say this moment that I will not die, not till ages hence, not till the world is exhausted? Let other men die, if they choose, or yield; let him that is strong enough live!"

After this flush of heroic mood, however, the glow subsided, and poor Septimius spent the rest of the day, as was his wont, poring over his books, in which all the meanings seemed dead and mouldy, and like pressed leaves (some of which dropped out of the books as he opened them), brown, brittle, sapless; so even the thoughts, which when the writers had gathered them seemed to them so brightly colored and full of life. Then he began to see that there must have been some principle of life left out of the book, so that these gathered thoughts lacked something that had given them their only value. Then he suspected that the way truly to live and answer the purposes of life was not to gather up thoughts into books, where they grew so dry, but to live and still be going about, full of green wisdom, ripening ever, not in maxims cut and dry, but a wisdom ready for daily occasions, like a living fountain; and that to be this, it was necessary to exist long on earth, drink in all its lessons, and not to die on the attainment of some smattering of truth; but to live all the more for that; and apply it to mankind and increase it thereby.

Everything drifted towards the strong, strange eddy into which his mind had been drawn: all his thoughts set hitherward.

So he sat brooding in his study until the shrill-voiced old woman–an aunt, who was his housekeeper and domestic ruler–called him to dinner,–a frugal dinner,–and chided him for seeming inattentive to a dish of early dandelions which she had gathered for him; but yet tempered her severity with respect for the future clerical rank of her nephew, and for his already being a bachelor of arts. The old woman's voice spoke outside of Septimius, rambling away, and he paying little heed, till at last dinner was over, and Septimius drew back his chair, about to leave the table.

"Nephew Septimius," said the old woman, "you began this meal to-day without asking a blessing, you get up from it without giving thanks, and you soon to be a minister of the Word."

"God bless the meat," replied Septimius (by way of blessing), "and make it strengthen us for the life he means us to bear. Thank God for our food," he added (by way of grace), "and may it become a portion in us of an immortal body."

"That sounds good, Septimius," said the old lady. "Ah! you'll be a mighty man in the pulpit, and worthy to keep up the name of your great-grandfather, who, they say, made the leaves wither on a tree with the fierceness of his blast against a sin. Some say, to be sure, it was an early frost that helped him."

"I never heard that before, Aunt Keziah," said Septimius.

"I warrant you no," replied his aunt. "A man dies, and his greatness perishes as if it had never been, and people remember nothing of him only when they see his gravestone over his old dry bones, and say he was a good man in his day."

"What truth there is in Aunt Keziah's words!" exclaimed Septimius. "And how I hate the thought and anticipation of that contemptuous appreciation of a man after his death! Every living man triumphs over every dead one, as he lies, poor and helpless, under the mould, a pinch of dust, a heap of bones, an evil odor! I hate the thought! It shall not be so!"

It was strange how every little incident thus brought him back to that one subject which was taking so strong hold of his mind; every avenue led thitherward; and he took it for an indication that nature had intended, by innumerable ways, to point out to us the great truth that death was an alien misfortune, a prodigy, a monstrosity, into which man had only fallen by defect; and that even now, if a man had a reasonable portion of his original strength in him, he might live forever and spurn death.

Our story is an internal one, dealing as little as possible with outward events, and taking hold of these only where it cannot be helped, in order by means of them to delineate the history of a mind bewildered in certain errors. We would not willingly, if we could, give a lively and picturesque surrounding to this delineation, but it is necessary that we should advert to the circumstances of the time in which this inward history was passing. We will say, therefore, that that night there was a cry of alarm passing all through the succession of country towns and rural communities that lay around Boston, and dying away towards the coast and the wilder forest borders. Horsemen galloped past the line of farm-houses shouting alarm! alarm! There were stories of marching troops coming like dreams through the midnight. Around the little rude meeting-houses there was here and there the beat of a drum, and the assemblage of farmers with their weapons. So all that night there was marching, there was mustering, there was trouble; and, on the road from Boston, a steady march of soldiers' feet onward, onward into the land whose last warlike disturbance had been when the red Indians trod it.

Septimius heard it, and knew, like the rest, that it was the sound of coming war. "Fools that men are!" said he, as he rose from bed and looked out at the misty stars; "they do not live long enough to know the value and purport of life, else they would combine together to live long, instead of throwing away the lives of thousands as they do. And what matters a little tyranny in so short a life? What matters a form of government for such ephemeral creatures?"

As morning brightened, these sounds, this clamor,—or something that was in the air and caused the clamor,—grew so loud that Septimius seemed to feel it even in his solitude. It was in the atmosphere,—storm, wild excitement, a coming deed. Men hurried along the usually lonely road in groups, with weapons in their hands,—the old fowling-piece of seven-foot barrel, with which the Puritans had shot ducks on the river and Walden Pond; the heavy harquebus, which perhaps had levelled one of King Philip's Indians; the old King gun, that blazed away at the French of Louisburg or Quebec,—hunter, husbandman, all were hurrying each other. It was a good time, everybody felt, to be alive, a nearer kindred, a closer sympathy between man and man; a sense of the goodness of the world, of the sacredness of country, of the excellence of life; and yet its slight account compared with any truth, any principle; the weighing of the material and ethereal, and the finding the former not worth considering, when, nevertheless, it had so much to do with the settlement of the crisis. The ennobling of brute force; the feeling that it had its godlike side; the drawing of heroic breath amid the scenes of ordinary life, so that it seemed as if they had all been transfigured since yesterday. Oh, high, heroic, tremulous juncture, when man felt himself almost an angel; on the verge of doing deeds that outwardly look so fiendish! Oh, strange rapture of the coming battle! We know something of that time now; we that have seen the muster of the village soldiery on the meeting-house green, and at railway stations; and heard the drum and fife, and seen the farewells; seen the familiar faces that we hardly knew, now that we felt them to be heroes; breathed higher breath for their sakes; felt our eyes moistened; thanked them in our souls for teaching us that nature is yet capable of heroic moments; felt how a great impulse lifts up a people, and every cold, passionless, indifferent spectator,—lifts him up into religion, and makes him join in what becomes an act of devotion, a prayer, when perhaps he but half approves.

Septimius could not study on a morning like this. He tried to say to himself that he had nothing to do with this excitement; that his studious life kept him away from it; that his intended profession was that of peace; but say

26

what he might to himself, there was a tremor, a bubbling impulse, a tingling in his ears,—the page that he opened glimmered and dazzled before him.

"Septimius! Septimius!" cried Aunt Keziah, looking into the room, "in Heaven's name, are you going to sit here to-day, and the redcoats coming to burn the house over our heads? Must I sweep you out with the broomstick? For shame, boy! for shame!"

"Are they coming, then, Aunt Keziah?" asked her nephew. "Well, I am not a fighting-man."

"Certain they are. They have sacked Lexington, and slain the people, and burnt the meeting-house. That concerns even the parsons; and you reckon yourself among them. Go out, go out, I say, and learn the news!"

Whether moved by these exhortations, or by his own stifled curiosity, Septimius did at length issue from his door, though with that reluctance which hampers and impedes men whose current of thought and interest runs apart from that of the world in general; but forth he came, feeling strangely, and yet with a strong impulse to fling himself headlong into the emotion of the moment. It was a beautiful morning, spring-like and summer-like at once. If there had been nothing else to do or think of, such a morning was enough for life only to breathe its air and be conscious of its inspiring influence.

Septimius turned along the road towards the village, meaning to mingle with the crowd on the green, and there learn all he could of the rumors that vaguely filled the air, and doubtless were shaping themselves into various forms of fiction.

As he passed the small dwelling of Rose Garfield, she stood on the doorstep, and bounded forth a little way to meet him, looking frightened, excited, and yet half pleased, but strangely pretty; prettier than ever before, owing to some hasty adornment or other, that she would never have succeeded so well in giving to herself if she had had more time to do it in.

"Septimius—Mr. Felton," cried she, asking information of him who, of all men in the neighborhood, knew nothing of the intelligence afloat; but it showed a certain importance that Septimius had with her. "Do you really think the redcoats are coming? Ah, what shall we do? What shall we do? But you are not going to the village, too, and leave us all alone?"

"I know not whether they are coming or no, Rose," said Septimius, stopping to admire the young girl's fresh beauty, which made a double stroke upon him by her excitement, and, moreover, made her twice as free with him as ever she had been before; for there is nothing truer than that any breaking up of the ordinary state of things is apt to shake women out of their proprieties, break down barriers, and bring them into perilous proximity with the world. "Are you alone here? Had you not better take shelter in the village?"

"And leave my poor, bedridden grandmother!" cried Rose, angrily. "You know I can't, Septimius. But I suppose I am in no danger. Go to the village, if you like."

"Where is Robert Hagburn?" asked Septimius.

"Gone to the village this hour past, with his grandfather's old firelock on his shoulder," said Rose; "he was running bullets before daylight."

"Rose, I will stay with you," said Septimius.

"Oh gracious, here they come, I'm sure!" cried Rose. "Look yonder at the dust. Mercy! a man at a gallop!"

In fact, along the road, a considerable stretch of which was visible, they heard the clatter of hoofs and saw a little cloud of dust approaching at the rate of a gallop, and disclosing, as it drew near, a hatless countryman in his shirt-sleeves, who, bending over his horse's neck, applied a cart-whip lustily to the animal's flanks, so as to incite him to most unwonted speed. At the same time, glaring upon Rose and Septimius, he lifted up his voice and shouted in a strange, high tone, that communicated the tremor and excitement of the shouter to each auditor: "Alarum! alarum! alarum! The redcoats! The redcoats! To arms! alarum!"

And trailing this sound far wavering behind him like a pennon, the eager horseman dashed onward to the village.

"Oh dear, what shall we do?" cried Rose, her eyes full of tears, yet dancing with excitement. "They are coming! they are coming! I hear the drum and fife."

"I really believe they are," said Septimius, his cheek flushing and growing pale, not with fear, but the inevitable tremor, half painful, half pleasurable, of the moment. "Hark! there was the shrill note of a fife. Yes, they are coming!"

He tried to persuade Rose to hide herself in the house; but that young person would not be persuaded to do so, clinging to Septimius in a way that flattered while it perplexed him. Besides, with all the girl's fright, she had still a good deal of courage, and much curiosity too, to see what these redcoats were of whom she heard such terrible stories.

"Well, well, Rose," said Septimius; "I doubt not we may stay here without danger,–you, a woman, and I, whose profession is to be that of peace and good-will to all men. They cannot, whatever is said of them, be on an errand of massacre. We will stand here quietly; and, seeing that we do not fear them, they will understand that we mean them no harm."

They stood, accordingly, a little in front of the door by the well-curb, and soon they saw a heavy cloud of dust, from amidst which shone bayonets; and anon, a military band, which had hitherto been silent, struck up, with drum and fife, to which the tramp of a thousand feet fell in regular order; then came the column, moving massively, and the redcoats who seemed somewhat wearied by a long night-march, dusty, with bedraggled gaiters, covered with sweat which had rundown from their powdered locks. Nevertheless, these ruddy, lusty Englishmen marched stoutly, as men that needed only a half-hour's rest, a good breakfast, and a pot of beer apiece, to make them ready to face the world. Nor did their faces look anywise rancorous; but at most, only heavy, cloddish, good-natured, and humane.

"O heavens, Mr. Felton!" whispered Rose, "why should we shoot these men, or they us? they look kind, if homely. Each of them has a mother and sisters, I suppose, just like our men."

"It is the strangest thing in the world that we can think of killing them," said Septimius. "Human life is so precious."

Just as they were passing the cottage, a halt was called by the commanding officer, in order that some little rest might get the troops into a better condition and give them breath before entering the village, where it was important to make as imposing a show as possible. During this brief stop, some of the soldiers approached the well-curb, near which Rose and Septimius were standing, and let down the bucket to satisfy their thirst. A young officer, a petulant boy, extremely handsome, and of gay and buoyant deportment, also came up.

"Get me a cup, pretty one," said he, patting Rose's cheek with great freedom, though it was somewhat and indefinitely short of rudeness; "a mug, or something to drink out of, and you shall have a kiss for your pains."

"Stand off, sir!" said Septimius, fiercely; "it is a coward's part to insult a woman."

"I intend no insult in this," replied the handsome young officer, suddenly snatching a kiss from Rose, before she could draw back. "And if you think it so, my good friend, you had better take your weapon and get as much satisfaction as you can, shooting at me from behind a hedge."

Before Septimius could reply or act,—and, in truth, the easy presumption of the young Englishman made it difficult for him, an inexperienced recluse as he was, to know what to do or say,—the drum beat a little tap, recalling the soldiers to their rank and to order. The young officer hastened back, with a laughing glance at Rose, and a light, contemptuous look of defiance at Septimius, the drums rattling out in full beat, and the troops marched on.

"What impertinence!" said Rose, whose indignant color made her look pretty enough almost to excuse the offence.

It is not easy to see how Septimius could have shielded her from the insult; and yet he felt inconceivably outraged and humiliated at the thought that this offence had occurred while Rose was under his protection, and he responsible for her. Besides, somehow or other, he was angry with her for having undergone the wrong, though certainly most unreasonably; for the whole thing was quicker done than said.

"You had better go into the house now, Rose," said he, "and see to your bedridden grandmother."

"And what will you do, Septimius?" asked she.

"Perhaps I will house myself, also," he replied. "Perhaps take yonder proud redcoat's counsel, and shoot him behind a hedge."

"But not kill him outright; I suppose he has a mother and a sweetheart, the handsome young officer," murmured Rose pityingly to herself.

Septimius went into his house, and sat in his study for some hours, in that unpleasant state of feeling which a man of brooding thought is apt to experience when the world around him is in a state of intense action, which he finds it impossible to sympathize with. There seemed to be a stream rushing past him, by which, even if he plunged into the midst of it, he could not be wet. He felt himself strangely ajar with the human race, and would have given much either to be in full accord with it, or to be separated from it forever.

"I am dissevered from it. It is my doom to be only a spectator of life; to look on as one apart from it. Is it not well, therefore, that, sharing none of its pleasures and happiness, I should be free of its fatalities its brevity? How cold I am now, while this whirlpool of public feeling is eddying around me! It is as if I had not been born of woman!"

Thus it was that, drawing wild inferences from phenomena of the mind and heart common to people who, by some morbid action within themselves, are set ajar with the world, Septimius continued still to come round to that strange idea of undyingness which had recently taken possession of him. And yet he was wrong in thinking himself cold, and that he felt no sympathy in the fever of patriotism that was throbbing through his countrymen. He was restless as a flame; he could not fix his thoughts upon his book; he could not sit in his chair, but kept pacing to and fro, while through the open window came noises to which his imagination gave diverse interpretation. Now it was a distant drum; now shouts; by and by there came the rattle of musketry, that seemed to proceed from some point more distant than the village; a regular roll, then a ragged volley, then scattering shots. Unable any longer to preserve this unnatural indifference, Septimius snatched his gun, and, rushing out of the house, climbed the abrupt hill-side behind, whence he could see a long way towards the village, till a slight bend hid the uneven road. It was quite vacant, not a passenger upon it. But there seemed to be confusion in that direction; an unseen and inscrutable trouble, blowing thence towards him, intimated by vague sounds,—by no sounds. Listening eagerly, however, he at last fancied a mustering sound of the drum; then it seemed as if it were coming towards him; while in advance rode another horseman, the same kind of headlong messenger, in appearance, who had passed the house with his ghastly cry of alarum; then appeared scattered countrymen, with guns in their hands, straggling across fields. Then he caught sight of the regular array of British soldiers, filling the road with their front, and marching along as firmly as ever, though at a quick pace, while he fancied that the officers looked watchfully around. As he looked, a shot rang sharp from the hill-side towards the village; the smoke curled up, and Septimius saw a man stagger and fall in the midst of the troops. Septimius shuddered; it was so like murder that he really could not tell the difference; his knees trembled beneath him; his breath grew short, not with terror, but with some new sensation of awe.

Another shot or two came almost simultaneously from the wooded height, but without any effect that Septimius could perceive. Almost at the same moment a company of the British soldiers wheeled from the main body, and, dashing out of the road, climbed the hill, and disappeared into the wood and shrubbery that veiled it. There were a few straggling shots, by whom fired, or with what effect, was invisible, and meanwhile the main body of the enemy proceeded along the road. They had now advanced so nigh that Septimius was strangely assailed by the idea that he might, with the gun in his hand, fire right into the midst of them, and select any man of that now hostile band to be a victim. How strange, how strange it is, this deep, wild passion that nature has implanted in us to be the death of our fellow-creatures, and which coexists at the same time with horror! Septimius levelled his weapon, and drew it up again; he marked a mounted officer, who seemed to be in chief command, whom he knew that he could kill. But no! he had really no such purpose. Only it was such a temptation. And in a moment the horse would leap, the officer would fall and lie there in the dust of the road, bleeding, gasping, breathing in spasms, breathing no more.

While the young man, in these unusual circumstances, stood watching the marching of the troops, he heard the noise of rustling boughs, and the voices of men, and soon understood that the party, which he had seen separate itself from the main body and ascend the hill, was now marching along on the hill-top, the long ridge which, with a gap or two, extended as much as a mile from the village. One of these gaps occurred a little way from where Septimius stood. They were acting as flank guard, to prevent the up-roused people from coming so close to the main body as to fire upon it. He looked and saw that the detachment of British was plunging down one side of this gap, with intent to ascend the other, so that they would pass directly over the spot where he stood; a slight removal to one side, among the small bushes, would conceal him. He stepped aside accordingly, and from his concealment, not without drawing quicker breaths, beheld the party draw near. They were more intent upon the space between them and the main body than upon the dense thicket of birch-trees, pitch-pines, sumach, and dwarf oaks, which, scarcely yet beginning to bud into leaf, lay on the other side, and in which Septimius lurked.

[Describe how their faces affected him, passing so near; how strange they seemed.]

They had all passed, except an officer who brought up the rear, and who had perhaps been attracted by some slight motion that Septimius made,– some rustle in the thicket; for he stopped, fixed his eyes piercingly towards the spot where he stood, and levelled a light fusil which he carried. "Stand out, or I shoot," said he.

Not to avoid the shot, but because his manhood felt a call upon it not to skulk in obscurity from an open enemy, Septimius at once stood forth, and confronted the same handsome young officer with whom those fierce words had passed on account of his rudeness to Rose Garfield. Septimius's fierce Indian blood stirred in him, and gave a murderous excitement.

"Ah, it is you!" said the young officer, with a haughty smile. "You meant, then, to take up with my hint of shooting at me from behind a hedge? This is better. Come, we have in the first place the great quarrel between me a king's soldier, and you a rebel; next our private affair, on account of yonder pretty girl. Come, let us take a shot on either score!"

The young officer was so handsome, so beautiful, in budding youth; there was such a free, gay petulance in his manner; there seemed so little of real evil in him; he put himself on equal ground with the rustic Septimius so generously, that the latter, often so morbid and sullen, never felt a greater kindness for fellow-man than at this moment for this youth.

"I have no enmity towards you," said he; "go in peace."

"No enmity!" replied the officer. "Then why were you here with your gun amongst the shrubbery? But I have a mind to do my first deed of arms on you; so give up your weapon, and come with me as prisoner."

"A prisoner!" cried Septimius, that Indian fierceness that was in him arousing itself, and thrusting up its malign head like a snake. "Never! If you would have me, you must take my dead body."

"Ah well, you have pluck in you, I see, only it needs a considerable stirring. Come, this is a good quarrel of ours. Let us fight it out. Stand where you are, and I will give the word of command. Now; ready, aim, fire!"

As the young officer spoke the three last words, in rapid succession, he and his antagonist brought their firelocks to the shoulder, aimed and fired. Septimius felt, as it were, the sting of a gadfly passing across his temple, as the Englishman's bullet grazed it; but, to his surprise and horror (for the whole thing scarcely seemed real to him), he saw the officer give a great start, drop his fusil, and stagger against a tree, with his hand to his breast. He endeavored to support himself erect, but, failing in the effort, beckoned to Septimius.

"Come, my good friend," said he, with that playful, petulant smile flitting over his face again. "It is my first and last fight. Let me down as softly as you can on mother earth, the mother of both you and me; so we are brothers; and this may be a brotherly act, though it does not look so, nor feel so. Ah! that was a twinge indeed!"

"Good God!" exclaimed Septimius. "I had no thought of this, no malice towards you in the least!"

"Nor I towards you," said the young man. "It was boy's play, and the end of it is that I die a boy, instead of living forever, as perhaps I otherwise might."

"Living forever!" repeated Septimius, his attention arrested, even at that breathless moment, by words that rang so strangely on what had been his brooding thought.

"Yes; but I have lost my chance," said the young officer. Then, as Septimius helped him to lie against the little hillock of a decayed and buried stump, "Thank you; thank you. If you could only call back one of my comrades to hear my dying words. But I forgot. You have killed me, and they would take your life."

In truth, Septimius was so moved and so astonished, that he probably would have called back the young man's comrades, had it been possible; but, marching at the swift rate of men in peril, they had already gone far onward, in their passage through the shrubbery that had ceased to rustle behind them.

"Yes; I must die here!" said the young man, with a forlorn expression, as of a school-boy far away from home, "and nobody to see me now but you, who have killed me. Could you fetch me a drop of water? I have a great thirst."

Septimius, in a dream of horror and pity, rushed down the hill-side; the house was empty, for Aunt Keziah had gone for shelter and sympathy to some of the neighbors. He filled a jug with cold water, and hurried back to the hill-top, finding the young officer looking paler and more deathlike within those few moments.

"I thank you, my enemy that was, my friend that is," murmured he, faintly smiling. "Methinks, next to the father and mother that gave us birth, the next most intimate relation must be with the man that slays us, who introduces us to the mysterious world to which this is but the portal. You and I are singularly connected, doubt it not, in the scenes of the unknown world."

35

"Oh, believe me," cried Septimius, "I grieve for you like a brother!"

"I see it, my dear friend," said the young officer; "and though my blood is on your hands, I forgive you freely, if there is anything to forgive. But I am dying, and have a few words to say, which you must hear. You have slain me in fair fight, and my spoils, according to the rules and customs of warfare, belong to the victor. Hang up my sword and fusil over your chimney-place, and tell your children, twenty years hence, how they were won. My purse, keep it or give it to the poor. There is something, here next my heart, which I would fain have sent to the address which I will give you."

Septimius, obeying his directions, took from his breast a miniature that hung round it; but, on examination, it proved that the bullet had passed directly through it, shattering the ivory, so that the woman's face it represented was quite destroyed.

"Ah! that is a pity," said the young man; and yet Septimius thought that there was something light and contemptuous mingled with the pathos in his tones. "Well, but send it; cause it to be transmitted, according to the address."

He gave Septimius, and made him take down on a tablet which he had about him, the name of a hall in one of the midland counties of England.

"Ah, that old place," said he, "with its oaks, and its lawn, and its park, and its Elizabethan gables! I little thought I should die here, so far away, in this barren Yankee land. Where will you bury me?"

As Septimius hesitated to answer, the young man continued: "I would like to have lain in the little old church at Whitnash, which comes up before me now, with its low, gray tower, and the old yew-tree in front, hollow with age, and the village clustering about it, with its thatched houses. I would be loath to lie in one of your Yankee graveyards, for I have a distaste for them,— though I love you, my slayer. Bury me here, on this very spot. A soldier lies best where he falls."

"Here, in secret?" exclaimed Septimius.

"Yes; there is no consecration in your Puritan burial-grounds," said the dying youth, some of that queer narrowness of English Churchism coming into his mind. "So bury me here, in my soldier's dress. Ah! and my watch! I have done with time, and you, perhaps, have a long lease of it; so take it, not as spoil, but as my parting gift. And that reminds me of one other thing. Open that pocket-book which you have in your hand."

Septimius did so, and by the officer's direction took from one of its compartments a folded paper, closely written in a crabbed hand; it was considerably worn in the outer folds, but not within. There was also a small silver key in the pocket-book.

"I leave it with you," said the officer; "it was given me by an uncle, a learned man of science, who intended me great good by what he there wrote. Reap the profit, if you can. Sooth to say, I never read beyond the first lines of the paper."

Septimius was surprised, or deeply impressed, to see that through this paper, as well as through the miniature, had gone his fatal bullet,–straight through the midst; and some of the young man's blood, saturating his dress, had wet the paper all over. He hardly thought himself likely to derive any good from what it had cost a human life, taken (however uncriminally) by his own hands, to obtain.

"Is there anything more that I can do for you?" asked he, with genuine sympathy and sorrow, as he knelt by his fallen foe's side.

"Nothing, nothing, I believe," said he. "There was one thing I might have confessed; if there were a holy man here, I might have confessed, and asked his prayers; for though I have lived few years, it has been long enough to do a great wrong! But I will try to pray in my secret soul. Turn my face towards the trunk of the tree, for I have taken my last look at the world. There, let me be now."

Septimius did as the young man requested, and then stood leaning against one of the neighboring pines, watching his victim with a tender concern that made him feel as if the convulsive throes that passed through his frame were felt equally in his own. There was a murmuring from the youth's lips which seemed to Septimius swift, soft, and melancholy, like the voice of a child when it has some naughtiness to confess to its mother at bedtime; contrite, pleading, yet trusting. So it continued for a few minutes; then there was a sudden start and struggle, as if he were striving to rise; his eyes met those of Septimius with a wild, troubled gaze, but as the latter caught him in his arms, he was dead. Septimius laid the body softly down on the leaf-strewn earth, and tried, as he had heard was the custom with the dead, to compose the features distorted by the dying agony. He then flung himself on the ground at a little distance, and gave himself up to the reflections suggested by the strange occurrences of the last hour.

He had taken a human life; and, however the circumstances might excuse him,—might make the thing even something praiseworthy, and that would be called patriotic,—still, it was not at once that a fresh country youth could see anything but horror in the blood with which his hand was stained. It seemed so dreadful to have reduced this gay, animated, beautiful being to a lump of dead flesh for the flies to settle upon, and which in a few hours would begin to decay; which must be put forthwith into the earth, lest it should be a horror to men's eyes; that delicious beauty for woman to love; that strength and courage to make him famous among men,—all come to nothing; all probabilities of life in one so gifted; the renown, the position, the pleasures, the profits, the keen ecstatic joy,—this never could be made up,—all ended quite; for the dark doubt descended upon Septimius, that, because of the very fitness that was in this youth to enjoy this world, so much the less chance was thereof his being fit for any other world. What could it do for him there,—this beautiful grace and elegance of feature,—where there was no form, nothing tangible nor visible? what good that readiness and aptness for associating with all created things, doing his part, acting, enjoying, when, under the changed conditions of another state of being, all this adaptedness would fail? Had he been gifted with permanence on earth, there could not have been a more admirable creature than this young man; but as his fate had turned out, he was a mere grub, an illusion, something that nature had held out in mockery, and then withdrawn. A weed might grow from his dust now; that little spot on the barren hill-top, where he had desired to be buried, would be greener for some years to come, and that was all the difference. Septimius could not get beyond the earthiness; his feeling was as if, by an act of violence, he had forever cut off a happy human existence. And such was his own love of life and clinging to it, peculiar to dark, sombre natures, and which lighter and gayer ones can never know, that he shuddered at his deed, and at himself, and could with difficulty bear to be alone with the corpse of his victim,–trembled at the thought of turning his face towards him.

Yet he did so, because he could not endure the imagination that the dead youth was turning his eyes towards him as he lay; so he came and stood beside him, looking down into his white, upturned face. But it was wonderful! What a change had come over it since, only a few moments ago, he looked at that death-contorted countenance! Now there was a high and sweet expression upon it, of great joy and surprise, and yet a quietude diffused throughout, as if the peace being so very great was what had surprised him. The expression was like a light gleaming and glowing within him. Septimius had often, at a certain space of time after sunset, looking westward, seen a living radiance in the sky,–the last light of the dead day that seemed just the counterpart of this death-light in the young man's face. It was as if the youth were just at the gate of heaven, which, swinging softly open, let the inconceivable glory of the blessed city shine upon his face, and kindle it up with gentle, undisturbing astonishment and purest joy. It was an expression contrived by God's providence to comfort; to overcome all the dark auguries that the physical ugliness of death inevitably creates, and to prove by the divine glory on the face, that the ugliness is a delusion. It was as if the dead man himself showed his face out of the sky, with heaven's blessing on it, and bade the afflicted be of good cheer, and believe in immortality.

Septimius remembered the young man's injunctions to bury him there, on the hill, without uncovering the body; and though it seemed a sin and shame to cover up that beautiful body with earth of the grave, and give it to the worm, yet he resolved to obey.

Be it confessed that, beautiful as the dead form looked, and guiltless as Septimius must be held in causing his death, still he felt as if he should be eased when it was under the ground. He hastened down to the house, and brought up a shovel and a pickaxe, and began his unwonted task of grave-digging, delving earnestly a deep pit, sometimes pausing in his toil, while the sweat-drops poured from him, to look at the beautiful clay that was to occupy it. Sometimes he paused, too, to listen to the shots that pealed in the far distance, towards the east, whither the battle had long since rolled out of reach and almost out of hearing. It seemed to have gathered about itself the whole life of the land, attending it along its bloody course in a struggling throng of shouting, shooting men, so still and solitary was everything left behind it. It seemed the very midland solitude of the world where Septimius was delving at the grave. He and his dead were alone together, and he was going to put the body under the sod, and be quite alone.

The grave was now deep, and Septimius was stooping down into its depths among dirt and pebbles, levelling off the bottom, which he considered to be profound enough to hide the young man's mystery forever, when a voice spoke above him; a solemn, quiet voice, which he knew well.

"Septimius! what are you doing here?"

He looked up and saw the minister.

"I have slain a man in fair fight," answered he, "and am about to bury him as he requested. I am glad you are come. You, reverend sir, can fitly say a prayer at his obsequies. I am glad for my own sake; for it is very lonely and terrible to be here."

He climbed out of the grave, and, in reply to the minister's inquiries, communicated to him the events of the morning, and the youth's strange wish to be buried here, without having his remains subjected to the hands of those who would prepare it for the grave. The minister hesitated.

"At an ordinary time," said he, "such a singular request would of course have to be refused. Your own safety, the good and wise rules that make it necessary that all things relating to death and burial should be done publicly and in order, would forbid it."

"Yes," replied Septimius; "but, it may be, scores of men will fall to-day, and be flung into hasty graves without funeral rites; without its ever being known, perhaps, what mother has lost her son. I cannot but think that I ought to perform the dying request of the youth whom I have slain. He trusted in me not to uncover his body myself, nor to betray it to the hands of others."

"A singular request," said the good minister, gazing with deep interest at the beautiful dead face, and graceful, slender, manly figure. "What could have been its motive? But no matter. I think, Septimius, that you are bound to obey his request; indeed, having promised him, nothing short of an impossibility should prevent your keeping your faith. Let us lose no time, then."

With few but deeply solemn rites the young stranger was laid by the minister and the youth who slew him in his grave. A prayer was made, and then Septimius, gathering some branches and twigs, spread them over the face that was turned upward from the bottom of the pit, into which the sun gleamed downward, throwing its rays so as almost to touch it. The twigs partially hid it, but still its white shone through. Then the minister threw a handful of earth upon it, and, accustomed as he was to burials, tears fell from his eyes along with the mould.

"It is sad," said he, "this poor young man, coming from opulence, no doubt, a dear English home, to die here for no end, one of the first-fruits of a bloody war,–so much privately sacrificed. But let him rest, Septimius. I am sorry that he fell by your hand, though it involves no shadow of a crime. But death is a thing too serious not to melt into the nature of a man like you."

"It does not weigh upon my conscience, I think," said Septimius; "though I cannot but feel sorrow, and wish my hand were as clean as yesterday. It is, indeed, a dreadful thing to take human life."

"It is a most serious thing," replied the minister; "but perhaps we are apt to over-estimate the importance of death at any particular moment. If the question were whether to die or to live forever, then, indeed, scarcely anything should justify the putting a fellow-creature to death. But since it only shortens his earthly life, and brings a little forward a change which, since God permits it, is, we may conclude, as fit to take place then as at any other time, it alters the case. I often think that there are many things that occur to us in our daily life, many unknown crises, that are more important to us than this mysterious circumstance of death, which we deem the most important of all. All we understand of it is, that it takes the dead person away from our knowledge of him, which, while we live with him, is so very scanty."

"You estimate at nothing, it seems, his earthly life, which might have been so happy."

"At next to nothing," said the minister; "since, as I have observed, it must, at any rate, have closed so soon."

Septimius thought of what the young man, in his last moments, had said of his prospect or opportunity of living a life of interminable length, and which prospect he had bequeathed to himself. But of this he did not speak to the minister, being, indeed, ashamed to have it supposed that he would put any serious weight on such a bequest, although it might be that the dark enterprise of his nature had secretly seized upon this idea, and, though yet sane enough to be influenced by a fear of ridicule, was busy incorporating it with his thoughts.

So Septimius smoothed down the young stranger's earthy bed, and returned to his home, where he hung up the sword over the mantel-piece in his study, and hung the gold watch, too, on a nail,—the first time he had ever had possession of such a thing. Nor did he now feel altogether at ease in his mind about keeping it,—the time-measurer of one whose mortal life he had cut off. A splendid watch it was, round as a turnip. There seems to be a natural right in one who has slain a man to step into his vacant place in all respects; and from the beginning of man's dealings with man this right has been practically recognized, whether among warriors or robbers, as paramount to every other. Yet Septimius could not feel easy in availing himself of this right. He therefore resolved to keep the watch, and even the sword and fusil,—which were less questionable spoils of war,—only till he should be able to restore them to some representative of the young officer. The contents of the purse, in accordance with the request of the dying youth, he would expend in relieving the necessities of those whom the war (now broken out, and of which no one could see the limit) might put in need of it. The miniature, with its broken and shattered face, that had so vainly interposed itself between its wearer and death, had been sent to its address.

But as to the mysterious document, the written paper, that he had laid aside without unfolding it, but with a care that betokened more interest in it than in either gold or weapon, or even in the golden representative of that earthly time on which he set so high a value. There was something tremulous in his touch of it; it seemed as if he were afraid of it by the mode in which he hid it away, and secured himself from it, as it were.

This done, the air of the room, the low-ceilinged eastern room where he studied and thought, became too close for him, and he hastened out; for he was full of the unshaped sense of all that had befallen, and the perception of the great public event of a broken-out war was intermixed with that of what he had done personally in the great struggle that was beginning. He longed, too, to know what was the news of the battle that had gone rolling onward along the hitherto peaceful country road, converting everywhere (this demon of war, we mean), with one blast of its red sulphurous breath, the peaceful husbandman to a soldier thirsting for blood. He turned his steps, therefore, towards the village, thinking it probable that news must have arrived either of defeat or victory, from messengers or fliers, to cheer or sadden the old men, the women, and the children, who alone perhaps remained there.

But Septimius did not get to the village. As he passed along by the cottage that has been already described, Rose Garfield was standing at the door, peering anxiously forth to know what was the issue of the conflict,—as it has been woman's fate to do from the beginning of the world, and is so still. Seeing Septimius, she forgot the restraint that she had hitherto kept herself under, and, flying at him like a bird, she cried out, "Septimius, dear Septimius, where have you been? What news do you bring? You look as if you had seen some strange and dreadful thing."

"Ah, is it so? Does my face tell such stories?" exclaimed the young man. "I did not mean it should. Yes, Rose, I have seen and done such things as change a man in a moment."

"Then you have been in this terrible fight," said Rose.

"Yes, Rose, I have had my part in it," answered Septimius.

He was on the point of relieving his overburdened mind by telling her what had happened no farther off than on the hill above them; but, seeing her excitement, and recollecting her own momentary interview with the young officer, and the forced intimacy and link that had been established between them by the kiss, he feared to agitate her further by telling her that that gay and beautiful young man had since been slain, and deposited in a bloody grave by his hands. And yet the recollection of that kiss caused a thrill of vengeful joy at the thought that the perpetrator had since expiated his offence with his life, and that it was himself that did it, so deeply was Septimius's Indian nature of revenge and blood incorporated with that of more peaceful forefathers, although Septimius had grace enough to chide down that bloody spirit, feeling that it made him, not a patriot, but a murderer.

"Ah," said Rose, shuddering, "it is awful when we must kill one another! And who knows where it will end?"

"With me it will end here, Rose," said Septimius. "It may be lawful for any man, even if he have devoted himself to God, or however peaceful his pursuits, to fight to the death when the enemy's step is on the soil of his home; but only for that perilous juncture, which passed, he should return to his own way of peace. I have done a terrible thing for once, dear Rose, one that might well trace a dark line through all my future life; but henceforth I cannot think it my duty to pursue any further a work for which my studies and my nature unfit me."

"Oh no! Oh no!" said Rose; "never! and you a minister, or soon to be one. There must be some peacemakers left in the world, or everything will turn to blood and confusion; for even women grow dreadfully fierce in these times. My old grandmother laments her bedriddenness, because, she says, she cannot go to cheer on the people against the enemy. But she remembers the old times of the Indian wars, when the women were as much in danger of death as the men, and so were almost as fierce as they, and killed men sometimes with their own hands. But women, nowadays, ought to be gentler; let the men be fierce, if they must, except you, and such as you, Septimius."

"Ah, dear Rose," said Septimius, "I have not the kind and sweet impulses that you speak of. I need something to soften and warm my cold, hard life; something to make me feel how dreadful this time of warfare is. I need you, dear Rose, who are all kindness of heart and mercy."

And here Septimius, hurried away by I know not what excitement of the time,–the disturbed state of the country, his own ebullition of passion, the deed he had done, the desire to press one human being close to his life, because he had shed the blood of another, his half-formed purposes, his shapeless impulses; in short, being affected by the whole stir of his nature,– spoke to Rose of love, and with an energy that, indeed, there was no resisting when once it broke bounds. And Rose, whose maiden thoughts, to say the truth, had long dwelt upon this young man,–admiring him for a certain dark beauty, knowing him familiarly from childhood, and yet having the sense, that is so bewitching, of remoteness, intermixed with intimacy, because he was so unlike herself; having a woman's respect for scholarship, her imagination the more impressed by all in him that she could not comprehend,–Rose yielded to his impetuous suit, and gave him the troth that he requested. And yet it was with a sort of reluctance and drawing back; her whole nature, her secretest heart, her deepest womanhood, perhaps, did not consent. There was something in Septimius, in his wild, mixed nature, the monstrousness that had grown out of his hybrid race, the black infusions, too, which melancholic men had left there, the devilishness that had been symbolized in the popular regard about his family, that made her shiver, even while she came the closer to him for that very dread. And when he gave her the kiss of betrothment her lips grew white. If it had not been in the day of turmoil, if he had asked her in any quiet time, when Rose's heart was in its natural mood, it may well be that, with tears and pity for him, and half-pity for herself, Rose would have told Septimius that she did not think she could love him well enough to be his wife.

And how was it with Septimius? Well; there was a singular correspondence in his feelings to those of Rose Garfield. At first, carried away by a passion that seized him all unawares, and seemed to develop itself all in a moment, he felt, and so spoke to Rose, so pleaded his suit, as if his whole earthly happiness depended on her consent to be his bride. It seemed to him that her love would be the sunshine in the gloomy dungeon of his life. But when her bashful, downcast, tremulous consent was given, then immediately came a strange misgiving into his mind. He felt as if he had taken to himself something good and beautiful doubtless in itself, but which might be the exchange for one more suited to him, that he must now give up. The intellect, which was the prominent point in Septimius, stirred and heaved, crying out vaguely that its own claims, perhaps, were ignored in this contract. Septimius had perhaps no right to love at all; if he did, it should have been a woman of another make, who could be his intellectual companion and helper. And then, perchance,–perchance,–there was destined for him some high, lonely path, in which, to make any progress, to come to any end, he must walk unburdened by the affections. Such thoughts as these depressed and chilled (as many men have found them, or similar ones, to do) the moment of success that should have been the most exulting in the world. And so, in the kiss which these two lovers had exchanged there was, after all, something that repelled; and when they parted they wondered at their strange states of mind, but would not acknowledge that they had done a thing that ought not to have been done. Nothing is surer, however, than that, if we suffer ourselves to be drawn into too close proximity with people, if we over-estimate the degree of our proper tendency towards them, or theirs towards us, a reaction is sure to follow.

Septimius quitted Rose, and resumed his walk towards the village. But now it was near sunset, and there began to be straggling passengers along the road, some of whom came slowly, as if they had received hurts; all seemed wearied. Among them one form appeared which Rose soon found that she recognized. It was Robert Hagburn, with a shattered firelock in his hand, broken at the butt, and his left arm bound with a fragment of his shirt, and suspended in a handkerchief; and he walked weariedly, but brightened up at sight of Rose, as if ashamed to let her see how exhausted and dispirited he was. Perhaps he expected a smile, at least a more earnest reception than he met; for Rose, with the restraint of what had recently passed drawing her back, merely went gravely a few steps to meet him, and said, "Robert, how tired and pale you look! Are you hurt?"

"It is of no consequence," replied Robert Hagburn; "a scratch on my left arm from an officer's sword, with whose head my gunstock made instant acquaintance. It is no matter, Rose; you do not care for it, nor do I either."

"How can you say so, Robert?" she replied. But without more greeting he passed her, and went into his own house, where, flinging himself into a chair, he remained in that despondency that men generally feel after a fight, even if a successful one.

Septimius, the next day, lost no time in writing a letter to the direction given him by the young officer, conveying a brief account of the latter's death and burial, and a signification that he held in readiness to give up certain articles of property, at any future time, to his representatives, mentioning also the amount of money contained in the purse, and his intention, in compliance with the verbal will of the deceased, to expend it in alleviating the wants of prisoners. Having so done, he went up on the hill to look at the grave, and satisfy himself that the scene there had not been a dream; a point which he was inclined to question, in spite of the tangible evidence of the sword and watch, which still hung over the mantel-piece. There was the little mound, however, looking so incontrovertibly a grave, that it seemed to him as if all the world must see it, and wonder at the fact of its being there, and spend their wits in conjecturing who slept within; and, indeed, it seemed to give the affair a questionable character, this secret burial, and he wondered and wondered why the young man had been so earnest about it. Well; there was the grave; and, moreover, on the leafy earth, where the dying youth had lain, there were traces of blood, which no rain had yet washed away. Septimius wondered at the easiness with which he acquiesced in this deed; in fact, he felt in a slight degree the effects of that taste of blood, which makes the slaying of men, like any other abuse, sometimes become a passion. Perhaps it was his Indian trait stirring in him again; at any rate, it is not delightful to observe how readily man becomes a blood-shedding animal.

Looking down from the hill-top, he saw the little dwelling of Rose Garfield, and caught a glimpse of the girl herself, passing the windows or the door, about her household duties, and listened to hear the singing which usually broke out of her. But Rose, for some reason or other, did not warble as usual this morning. She trod about silently, and somehow or other she was translated out of the ideality in which Septimius usually enveloped her, and looked little more than a New England girl, very pretty indeed, but not enough so perhaps to engross a man's life and higher purposes into her own narrow circle; so, at least, Septimius thought. Looking a little farther,–down into the green recess where stood Robert Hagburn's house,–he saw that young man, looking very pale, with his arm in a sling sitting listlessly on a half-chopped log of wood which was not likely soon to be severed by Robert's axe. Like other lovers, Septimius had not failed to be aware that Robert Hagburn was sensible to Rose Garfield's attractions; and now, as he looked down on them both from his elevated position, he wondered if it would not have been better for Rose's happiness if her thoughts and virgin fancies had settled on that frank, cheerful, able, wholesome young man, instead of on himself, who met her on so few points; and, in relation to whom, there was perhaps a plant that had its root in the grave, that would entwine itself around his whole life, overshadowing it with dark, rich foliage and fruit that he alone could feast upon.

For the sombre imagination of Septimius, though he kept it as much as possible away from the subject, still kept hinting and whispering, still coming back to the point, still secretly suggesting that the event of yesterday was to have momentous consequences upon his fate.

He had not yet looked at the paper which the young man bequeathed to him; he had laid it away unopened; not that he felt little interest in it, but, on the contrary, because he looked for some blaze of light which had been reserved for him alone. The young officer had been only the bearer of it to him, and he had come hither to die by his hand, because that was the readiest way by which he could deliver his message. How else, in the infinite chances of human affairs, could the document have found its way to its destined possessor? Thus mused Septimius, pacing to and fro on the level edge of his hill-top, apart from the world, looking down occasionally into it, and seeing its love and interest away from him; while Rose, it might be looking upward, saw occasionally his passing figure, and trembled at the nearness and remoteness that existed between them; and Robert Hagburn looked too, and wondered what manner of man it was who, having won Rose Garfield (for his instinct told him this was so), could keep that distance between her and him, thinking remote thoughts.

Yes; there was Septimius treading a path of his own on the hill-top; his feet began only that morning to wear it in his walking to and fro, sheltered from the lower world, except in occasional glimpses, by the birches and locusts that threw up their foliage from the hill-side. But many a year thereafter he continued to tread that path, till it was worn deep with his footsteps and trodden down hard; and it was believed by some of his superstitious neighbors that the grass and little shrubs shrank away from his path, and made it wider on that account; because there was something in the broodings that urged him to and fro along the path alien to nature and its productions. There was another opinion, too, that an invisible fiend, one of his relatives by blood, walked side by side with him, and so made the pathway wider than his single footsteps could have made it. But all this was idle, and was, indeed, only the foolish babble that hovers like a mist about men who withdraw themselves from the throng, and involve themselves in unintelligible pursuits and interests of their own. For the present, the small world, which alone knew of him, considered Septimius as a studious young man, who was fitting for the ministry, and was likely enough to do credit to the ministerial blood that he drew from his ancestors, in spite of the wild stream that the Indian priest had contributed; and perhaps none the worse, as a clergyman, for having an instinctive sense of the nature of the Devil from his traditionary claims to partake of his blood. But what strange interest there is in tracing out the first steps by which we enter on a career that influences our life; and this deep-worn pathway on the hill-top, passing and repassing by a grave, seemed to symbolize it in Septimius's case.

I suppose the morbidness of Septimius's disposition was excited by the circumstances which had put the paper into his possession. Had he received it by post, it might not have impressed him; he might possibly have looked over it with ridicule, and tossed it aside. But he had taken it from a dying man, and he felt that his fate was in it; and truly it turned out to be so. He waited for a fit opportunity to open it and read it; he put it off as if he cared nothing about it; perhaps it was because he cared so much. Whenever he had a happy time with Rose (and, moody as Septimius was, such happy moments came), he felt that then was not the time to look into the paper,–it was not to be read in a happy mood.

Once he asked Rose to walk with him on the hilltop.

"Why, what a path you have worn here, Septimius!" said the girl. "You walk miles and miles on this one spot, and get no farther on than when you started. That is strange walking!"

"I don't know, Rose; I sometimes think I get a little onward. But it is sweeter–yes, much sweeter, I find–to have you walking on this path here than to be treading it alone."

"I am glad of that," said Rose; "for sometimes, when I look up here, and see you through the branches, with your head bent down, and your hands clasped behind you, treading, treading, treading, always in one way, I wonder whether I am at all in your mind. I don't think, Septimius," added she, looking up in his face and smiling, "that ever a girl had just such a young man for a lover."

"No young man ever had such a girl, I am sure," said Septimius; "so sweet, so good for him, so prolific of good influences!"

"Ah, it makes me think well of myself to bring such a smile into your face! But, Septimius, what is this little hillock here so close to our path? Have you heaped it up here for a seat? Shall we sit down upon it for an instant?–for it makes me more tired to walk backward and forward on one path than to go straight forward a much longer distance."

"Well; but we will not sit down on this hillock," said Septimius, drawing her away from it. "Farther out this way, if you please, Rose, where we shall have a better view over the wide plain, the valley, and the long, tame ridge of hills on the other side, shutting it in like human life. It is a landscape that never tires, though it has nothing striking about it; and I am glad that there are no great hills to be thrusting themselves into my thoughts, and crowding out better things. It might be desirable, in some states of mind, to have a glimpse of water,—to have the lake that once must have covered this green valley,—because water reflects the sky, and so is like religion in life, the spiritual element."

"There is the brook running through it, though we do not see it," replied Rose; "a torpid little brook, to be sure; but, as you say, it has heaven in its bosom, like Walden Pond, or any wider one."

As they sat together on the hill-top, they could look down into Robert Hagburn's enclosure, and they saw him, with his arm now relieved from the sling, walking about, in a very erect manner, with a middle-aged man by his side, to whom he seemed to be talking and explaining some matter. Even at that distance Septimius could see that the rustic stoop and uncouthness had somehow fallen away from Robert, and that he seemed developed.

"What has come to Robert Hagburn?" said he. "He looks like another man than the lout I knew a few weeks ago."

"Nothing," said Rose Garfield, "except what comes to a good many young men nowadays. He has enlisted, and is going to the war. It is a pity for his mother."

"A great pity," said Septimius. "Mothers are greatly to be pitied all over the country just now, and there are some even more to be pitied than the mothers, though many of them do not know or suspect anything about their cause of grief at present."

"Of whom do you speak?" asked Rose.

"I mean those many good and sweet young girls," said Septimius, "who would have been happy wives to the thousands of young men who now, like Robert Hagburn, are going to the war. Those young men—many of them at least—will sicken and die in camp, or be shot down, or struck through with bayonets on battle-fields, and turn to dust and bones; while the girls that would have loved them, and made happy firesides for them, will pine and wither, and tread along many sour and discontented years, and at last go out of life without knowing what life is. So you see, Rose, every shot that takes effect kills two at least, or kills one and worse than kills the other."

"No woman will live single on account of poor Robert Hagburn being shot," said Rose, with a change of tone; "for he would never be married were he to stay at home and plough the field."

"How can you tell that, Rose?" asked Septimius.

Rose did not tell how she came to know so much about Robert Hagburn's matrimonial purposes; but after this little talk it appeared as if something had risen up between them,—a sort of mist, a medium, in which their intimacy was not increased; for the flow and interchange of sentiment was balked, and they took only one or two turns in silence along Septimius's trodden path. I don't know exactly what it was; but there are cases in which it is inscrutably revealed to persons that they have made a mistake in what is of the highest concern to them; and this truth often comes in the shape of a vague depression of the spirit, like a vapor settling down on a landscape; a misgiving, coming and going perhaps, a lack of perfect certainty. Whatever it was, Rose and Septimius had no more tender and playful words that day; and Rose soon went to look after her grandmother, and Septimius went and shut himself up in his study, after making an arrangement to meet Rose the next day.

Septimius shut himself up, and drew forth the document which the young officer, with that singular smile on his dying face, had bequeathed to him as the reward of his death. It was in a covering of folded parchment, right through which, as aforesaid, was a bullet-hole and some stains of blood. Septimius unrolled the parchment cover, and found inside a manuscript, closely written in a crabbed hand; so crabbed, indeed, that Septimius could not at first read a word of it, nor even satisfy himself in what language it was written. There seemed to be Latin words, and some interspersed ones in Greek characters, and here and there he could doubtfully read an English sentence; but, on the whole, it was an unintelligible mass, conveying somehow an idea that it was the fruit of vast labor and erudition, emanating from a mind very full of books, and grinding and pressing down the great accumulation of grapes that it had gathered from so many vineyards, and squeezing out rich viscid juices,—potent wine,—with which the reader might get drunk. Some of it, moreover, seemed, for the further mystification of the officer, to be written in cipher; a needless precaution, it might seem, when the writer's natural chirography was so full of puzzle and bewilderment.

Septimius looked at this strange manuscript, and it shook in his hands as he held it before his eyes, so great was his excitement. Probably, doubtless, it was in a great measure owing to the way in which it came to him, with such circumstances of tragedy and mystery; as if–so secret and so important was it–it could not be within the knowledge of two persons at once, and therefore it was necessary that one should die in the act of transmitting it to the hand of another, the destined possessor, inheritor, profiter by it. By the bloody hand, as all the great possessions in this world have been gained and inherited, he had succeeded to the legacy, the richest that mortal man ever could receive. He pored over the inscrutable sentences, and wondered, when he should succeed in reading one, if it might summon up a subject-fiend, appearing with thunder and devilish demonstrations. And by what other strange chance had the document come into the hand of him who alone was fit to receive it? It seemed to Septimius, in his enthusiastic egotism, as if the whole chain of events had been arranged purposely for this end; a difference had come between two kindred peoples; a war had broken out; a young officer, with the traditions of an old family represented in his line, had marched, and had met with a peaceful student, who had been incited from high and noble motives to take his life; then came a strange, brief intimacy, in which his victim made the slayer his heir. All these chances, as they seemed, all these interferences of Providence, as they doubtless were, had been necessary in order to put this manuscript into the hands of Septimius, who now pored over it, and could not with certainty read one word!

But this did not trouble him, except for the momentary delay. Because he felt well assured that the strong, concentrated study that he would bring to it would remove all difficulties, as the rays of a lens melt stones; as the telescope pierces through densest light of stars, and resolves them into their individual brilliancies. He could afford to spend years upon it if it were necessary; but earnestness and application should do quickly the work of years.

Amid these musings he was interrupted by his Aunt Keziah; though generally observant enough of her nephew's studies, and feeling a sanctity in them, both because of his intending to be a minister and because she had a great reverence for learning, even if heathenish, this good old lady summoned Septimius somewhat peremptorily to chop wood for her domestic purposes. How strange it is,–the way in which we are summoned from all high purposes by these little homely necessities; all symbolizing the great fact that the earthly part of us, with its demands, takes up the greater portion of all our available force. So Septimius, grumbling and groaning, went to the woodshed and exercised himself for an hour as the old lady requested; and it was only by instinct that he worked, hardly conscious what he was doing. The whole of passing life seemed impertinent; or if, for an instant, it seemed otherwise, then his lonely speculations and plans seemed to become impalpable, and to have only the consistency of vapor, which his utmost concentration succeeded no further than to make into the likeness of absurd faces, mopping, mowing, and laughing at him.

But that sentence of mystic meaning shone out before him like a transparency, illuminated in the darkness of his mind; he determined to take it for his motto until he should be victorious in his quest. When he took his candle, to retire apparently to bed, he again drew forth the manuscript, and, sitting down by the dim light, tried vainly to read it; but he could not as yet settle himself to concentrated and regular effort; he kept turning the leaves of the manuscript, in the hope that some other illuminated sentence might gleam out upon him, as the first had done, and shed a light on the context around it; and that then another would be discovered, with similar effect, until the whole document would thus be illuminated with separate stars of light, converging and concentrating in one radiance that should make the whole visible. But such was his bad fortune, not another word of the manuscript was he able to read that whole evening; and, moreover, while he had still an inch of candle left, Aunt Keziah, in her nightcap,–as witch-like a figure as ever went to a wizard meeting in the forest with Septimius's ancestor,–appeared at the door of the room, aroused from her bed, and shaking her finger at him.

"Septimius," said she, "you keep me awake, and you will ruin your eyes, and turn your head, if you study till midnight in this manner. You'll never live to be a minister, if this is the way you go on."

"Well, well, Aunt Keziah," said Septimius, covering his manuscript with a book, "I am just going to bed now."

"Good night, then," said the old woman; "and God bless your labors."

Strangely enough, a glance at the manuscript, as he hid it from the old woman, had seemed to Septimius to reveal another sentence, of which he had imperfectly caught the purport; and when she had gone, he in vain sought the place, and vainly, too, endeavored to recall the meaning of what he had read. Doubtless his fancy exaggerated the importance of the sentence, and he felt as if it might have vanished from the book forever. In fact, the unfortunate young man, excited and tossed to and fro by a variety of unusual impulses, was got into a bad way, and was likely enough to go mad, unless the balancing portion of his mind proved to be of greater volume and effect than as yet appeared to be the case.

The next morning he was up, bright and early, poring over the manuscript with the sharpened wits of the new day, peering into its night, into its old, blurred, forgotten dream; and, indeed, he had been dreaming about it, and was fully possessed with the idea that, in his dream, he had taken up the inscrutable document, and read it off as glibly as he would the page of a modern drama, in a continual rapture with the deep truth that it made clear to his comprehension, and the lucid way in which it evolved the mode in which man might be restored to his originally undying state. So strong was the impression, that when he unfolded the manuscript, it was with almost the belief that the crabbed old handwriting would be plain to him. Such did not prove to be the case, however; so far from it, that poor Septimius in vain turned over the yellow pages in quest of the one sentence which he had been able, or fancied he had been able, to read yesterday. The illumination that had brought it out was now faded, and all was a blur, an inscrutableness, a scrawl of unintelligible characters alike. So much did this affect him, that he had almost a mind to tear it into a thousand fragments, and scatter it out of the window to the west-wind, that was then blowing past the house; and if, in that summer season, there had been a fire on the hearth, it is possible that easy realization of a destructive impulse might have incited him to fling the accursed scrawl into the hottest of the flames, and thus returned it to the Devil, who, he suspected, was the original author of it. Had he done so, what strange and gloomy passages would I have been spared the pain of relating! How different would have been the life of Septimius,–a thoughtful preacher of God's word, taking severe but conscientious views of man's state and relations, a heavy-browed walker and worker on earth, and, finally, a slumberer in an honored grave, with an epitaph bearing testimony to his great usefulness in his generation.

But, in the mean time, here was the troublesome day passing over him, and pestering, bewildering, and tripping him up with its mere sublunary troubles, as the days will all of us the moment we try to do anything that we flatter ourselves is of a little more importance than others are doing. Aunt Keziah tormented him a great while about the rich field, just across the road, in front of the house, which Septimius had neglected the cultivation of, unwilling to spare the time to plough, to plant, to hoe it himself, but hired a lazy lout of the village, when he might just as well have employed and paid wages to the scarecrow which Aunt Keziah dressed out in ancient habiliments, and set up in the midst of the corn. Then came an old codger from the village, talking to Septimius about the war,–a theme of which he was weary: telling the rumor of skirmishes that the next day would prove to be false, of battles that were immediately to take place, of encounters with the enemy in which our side showed the valor of twenty-fold heroes, but had to retreat; babbling about shells and mortars, battalions, manœuvres, angles, fascines, and other items of military art; for war had filled the whole brain of the people, and enveloped the whole thought of man in a mist of gunpowder.

In this way, sitting on his doorstep, or in the very study, haunted by such speculations, this wretched old man would waste the better part of a summer afternoon while Septimius listened, returning abstracted monosyllables, answering amiss, and wishing his persecutor jammed into one of the cannons he talked about, and fired off, to end his interminable babble in one roar; [talking] of great officers coming from France and other countries; of overwhelming forces from England, to put an end to the war at once; of the unlikelihood that it ever should be ended; of its hopelessness; of its certainty of a good and speedy end.

Then came limping along the lane a disabled soldier, begging his way home from the field, which, a little while ago, he had sought in the full vigor of rustic health he was never to know again; with whom Septimius had to talk, and relieve his wants as far as he could (though not from the poor young officer's deposit of English gold), and send him on his way.

Then came the minister to talk with his former pupil, about whom he had latterly had much meditation, not understanding what mood had taken possession of him; for the minister was a man of insight, and from conversations with Septimius, as searching as he knew how to make them, he had begun to doubt whether he were sufficiently sound in faith to adopt the clerical persuasion. Not that he supposed him to be anything like a confirmed unbeliever: but he thought it probable that these doubts, these strange, dark, disheartening suggestions of the Devil, that so surely infect certain temperaments and measures of intellect, were tormenting poor Septimius, and pulling him back from the path in which he was capable of doing so much good. So he came this afternoon to talk seriously with him, and to advise him, if the case were as he supposed, to get for a time out of the track of the thought in which he had so long been engaged; to enter into active life; and by and by, when the morbid influences should have been overcome by a change of mental and moral religion, he might return, fresh and healthy, to his original design.

"What can I do," asked Septimius, gloomily, "what business take up, when the whole land lies waste and idle, except for this war?"

"There is the very business, then," said the minister. "Do you think God's work is not to be done in the field as well as in the pulpit? You are strong, Septimius, of a bold character, and have a mien and bearing that gives you a natural command among men. Go to the wars, and do a valiant part for your country, and come back to your peaceful mission when the enemy has vanished. Or you might go as chaplain to a regiment, and use either hand in battle,—pray for success before a battle, help win it with sword or gun, and give thanks to God, kneeling on the bloody field, at its close. You have already stretched one foe on your native soil."

Septimius could not but smile within himself at this warlike and bloody counsel; and, joining it with some similar exhortations from Aunt Keziah, he was inclined to think that women and clergymen are, in matters of war, the most uncompromising and bloodthirsty of the community. However, he replied, coolly, that his moral impulses and his feelings of duty did not exactly impel him in this direction, and that he was of opinion that war was a business in which a man could not engage with safety to his conscience, unless his conscience actually drove him into it; and that this made all the difference between heroic battle and murderous strife. The good minister had nothing very effectual to answer to this, and took his leave, with a still stronger opinion than before that there was something amiss in his pupil's mind.

By this time, this thwarting day had gone on through its course of little and great impediments to his pursuit,—the discouragements of trifling and earthly business, of purely impertinent interruption, of severe and disheartening opposition from the powerful counteraction of different kinds of mind,—until the hour had come at which he had arranged to meet Rose Garfield. I am afraid the poor thwarted youth did not go to his love-tryst in any very amiable mood; but rather, perhaps, reflecting how all things earthly and immortal, and love among the rest, whichever category, of earth or heaven, it may belong to, set themselves against man's progress in any pursuit that he seeks to devote himself to. It is one struggle, the moment he undertakes such a thing, of everything else in the world to impede him.

However, as it turned out, it was a pleasant and happy interview that he had with Rose that afternoon. The girl herself was in a happy, tuneful mood, and met him with such simplicity, threw such a light of sweetness over his soul, that Septimius almost forgot all the wild cares of the day, and walked by her side with a quiet fulness of pleasure that was new to him. She reconciled him, in some secret way, to life as it was, to imperfection, to decay; without any help from her intellect, but through the influence of her character, she seemed, not to solve, but to smooth away, problems that troubled him; merely by being, by womanhood, by simplicity, she interpreted God's ways to him; she softened the stoniness that was gathering about his heart. And so they had a delightful time of talking, and laughing, and smelling to flowers; and when they were parting, Septimius said to her,–

"Rose, you have convinced me that this is a most happy world, and that Life has its two children, Birth and Death, and is bound to prize them equally; and that God is very kind to his earthly children; and that all will go well."

"And have I convinced you of all this?" replied Rose, with a pretty laughter. "It is all true, no doubt, but I should not have known how to argue for it. But you are very sweet, and have not frightened me to-day."

"Do I ever frighten you then, Rose?" asked Septimius, bending his black brow upon her with a look of surprise and displeasure.

"Yes, sometimes," said Rose, facing him with courage, and smiling upon the cloud so as to drive it away; "when you frown upon me like that, I am a little afraid you will beat me, all in good time."

"Now," said Septimius, laughing again, "you shall have your choice, to be beaten on the spot, or suffer another kind of punishment,–which?"

So saying, he snatched her to him, and strove to kiss her, while Rose, laughing and struggling, cried out, "The beating! the beating!" But Septimius relented not, though it was only Rose's cheek that he succeeded in touching. In truth, except for that first one, at the moment of their plighted troths, I doubt whether Septimius ever touched those soft, sweet lips, where the smiles dwelt and the little pouts. He now returned to his study, and questioned with himself whether he should touch that weary, ugly, yellow, blurred, unintelligible, bewitched, mysterious, bullet-penetrated, blood-stained manuscript again. There was an undefinable reluctance to do so, and at the same time an enticement (irresistible, as it proved) drawing him towards it. He yielded, and taking it from his desk, in which the precious, fatal treasure was locked up, he plunged into it again, and this time with a certain degree of success. He found the line which had before gleamed out, and vanished again, and which now started out in strong relief; even as when sometimes we see a certain arrangement of stars in the heavens, and again lose it, by not seeing its individual stars in the same relation as before; even so, looking at the manuscript in a different way, Septimius saw this fragment of a sentence, and saw, moreover, what was necessary to give it a certain meaning. "Set the root in a grave, and wait for what shall blossom. It will be very rich, and full of juice." This was the purport, he now felt sure, of the sentence he had lighted upon; and he took it to refer to the mode of producing something that was essential to the thing to be concocted. It might have only a moral being; or, as is generally the case, the moral and physical truth went hand in hand.

While Septimius was busying himself in this way, the summer advanced, and with it there appeared a new character, making her way into our pages. This was a slender and pale girl, whom Septimius was once startled to find, when he ascended his hill-top, to take his walk to and fro upon the accustomed path, which he had now worn deep.

What was stranger, she sat down close beside the grave, which none but he and the minister knew to be a grave; that little hillock, which he had levelled a little, and had planted with various flowers and shrubs; which the summer had fostered into richness, the poor young man below having contributed what he could, and tried to render them as beautiful as he might, in remembrance of his own beauty. Septimius wished to conceal the fact of its being a grave: not that he was tormented with any sense that he had done wrong in shooting the young man, which had been done in fair battle; but still it was not the pleasantest of thoughts, that he had laid a beautiful human creature, so fit for the enjoyment of life, there, when his own dark brow, his own troubled breast, might better, he could not but acknowledge, have been covered up there. [Perhaps there might sometimes be something fantastically gay in the language and behavior of the girl.]

Well; but then, on this flower and shrub-disguised grave, sat this unknown form of a girl, with a slender, pallid, melancholy grace about her, simply dressed in a dark attire, which she drew loosely about her. At first glimpse, Septimius fancied that it might be Rose; but it needed only a glance to undeceive him; her figure was of another character from the vigorous, though slight and elastic beauty of Rose; this was a drooping grace, and when he came near enough to see her face, he saw that those large, dark, melancholy eyes, with which she had looked at him, had never met his gaze before.

"Good-morrow, fair maiden," said Septimius, with such courtesy as he knew how to use (which, to say truth, was of a rustic order, his way of life having brought him little into female society). "There is a nice air here on the hill-top, this sultry morning below the hill!"

As he spoke, he continued to look wonderingly at the strange maiden, half fancying that she might be something that had grown up out of the grave; so unexpected she was, so simply unlike anything that had before come there.

The girl did not speak to him, but as she sat by the grave she kept weeding out the little white blades of faded autumn grass and yellow pine-spikes, peering into the soil as if to see what it was all made of, and everything that was growing there; and in truth, whether by Septimius's care or no, there seemed to be several kinds of flowers,–those little asters that abound everywhere, and golden flowers, such as autumn supplies with abundance. She seemed to be in quest of something, and several times plucked a leaf and examined it carefully; then threw it down again, and shook her head. At last she lifted up her pale face, and, fixing her eyes quietly on Septimius, spoke: "It is not here!"

A very sweet voice it was,–plaintive, low,–and she spoke to Septimius as if she were familiar with him, and had something to do with him. He was greatly interested, not being able to imagine who the strange girl was, or whence she came, or what, of all things, could be her reason for coming and sitting down by this grave, and apparently botanizing upon it, in quest of some particular plant.

"Are you in search of flowers?" asked Septimius. "This is but a barren spot for them, and this is not a good season. In the meadows, and along the margin of the watercourses, you might find the fringed gentian at this time. In the woods there are several pretty flowers,–the side-saddle flower, the anemone; violets are plentiful in spring, and make the whole hill-side blue. But this hill-top, with its soil strewn over a heap of pebble-stones, is no place for flowers."

"The soil is fit," said the maiden, "but the flower has not sprung up."

"What flower do you speak of?" asked Septimius.

"One that is not here," said the pale girl. "No matter. I will look for it again next spring."

"Do you, then, dwell hereabout?" inquired Septimius.

"Surely," said the maiden, with a look of surprise; "where else should I dwell? My home is on this hilltop."

It not a little startled Septimius, as may be supposed, to find his paternal inheritance, of which he and his forefathers had been the only owners since the world began (for they held it by an Indian deed), claimed as a home and abiding-place by this fair, pale, strange-acting maiden, who spoke as if she had as much right there as if she had grown up out of the soil like one of the wild, indigenous flowers which she had been gazing at and handling. However that might be, the maiden seemed now about to depart, rising, giving a farewell touch or two to the little verdant hillock, which looked much the neater for her ministrations.

"Are you going?" said Septimius, looking at her in wonder.

"For a time," said she.

"And shall I see you again?" asked he.

"Surely," said the maiden, "this is my walk, along the brow of the hill."

It again smote Septimius with a strange thrill of surprise to find the walk which he himself had made, treading it, and smoothing it, and beating it down with the pressure of his continual feet, from the time when the tufted grass made the sides all uneven, until now, when it was such a pathway as you may see through a wood, or over a field, where many feet pass every day,–to find this track and exemplification of his own secret thoughts and plans and emotions, this writing of his body, impelled by the struggle and movement of his soul, claimed as her own by a strange girl with melancholy eyes and voice, who seemed to have such a sad familiarity with him.

"You are welcome to come here," said he, endeavoring at least to keep such hold on his own property as was implied in making a hospitable surrender of it to another.

"Yes," said the girl, "a person should always be welcome to his own."

A faint smile seemed to pass over her face as she said this, vanishing, however, immediately into the melancholy of her usual expression. She went along Septimius's path, while he stood gazing at her till she reached the brow where it sloped towards Robert Hagburn's house; then she turned, and seemed to wave a slight farewell towards the young man, and began to descend. When her figure had entirely sunk behind the brow of the hill, Septimius slowly followed along the ridge, meaning to watch from that elevated station the course she would take; although, indeed, he would not have been surprised if he had seen nothing, no trace of her in the whole nearness or distance; in short, if she had been a freak, an illusion, of a hard-working mind that had put itself ajar by deeply brooding on abstruse matters, an illusion of eyes that he had tried too much by poring over the inscrutable manuscript, and of intellect that was mystified and bewildered by trying to grasp things that could not be grasped. A thing of witchcraft, a sort of fungus-growth out of the grave, an unsubstantiality altogether; although, certainly, she had weeded the grave with bodily fingers, at all events. Still he had so much of the hereditary mysticism of his race in him, that he might have held her supernatural, only that on reaching the brow of the hill he saw her feet approach the dwelling of Robert Hagburn's mother, who, moreover, appeared at the threshold beckoning her to come, with a motherly, hospitable air, that denoted she knew the strange girl, and recognized her as human.

It did not lessen Septimius's surprise, however, to think that such a singular being was established in the neighborhood without his knowledge; considered as a real occurrence of this world, it seemed even more unaccountable than if it had been a thing of ghostology and witchcraft. Continually through the day the incident kept introducing its recollection among his thoughts and studies; continually, as he paced along his path, this form seemed to hurry along by his side on the track that she had claimed for her own, and he thought of her singular threat or promise, whichever it were to be held, that he should have a companion there in future. In the decline of the day, when he met the schoolmistress coming home from her little seminary, he snatched the first opportunity to mention the apparition of the morning, and ask Rose if she knew anything of her.

"Very little," said Rose, "but she is flesh and blood, of that you may be quite sure. She is a girl who has been shut up in Boston by the siege; perhaps a daughter of one of the British officers, and her health being frail, she requires better air than they have there, and so permission was got for her, from General Washington, to come and live in the country; as any one may see, our liberties have nothing to fear from this poor brain-stricken girl. And Robert Hagburn, having to bring a message from camp to the selectmen here, had it in charge to bring the girl, whom his mother has taken to board."

"Then the poor thing is crazy?" asked Septimius.

"A little brain-touched, that is all," replied Rose, "owing to some grief that she has had; but she is quite harmless, Robert was told to say, and needs little or no watching, and will get a kind of fantastic happiness for herself, if only she is allowed to ramble about at her pleasure. If thwarted, she might be very wild and miserable."

"Have you spoken with her?" asked Septimius.

"A word or two this morning, as I was going to my school," said Rose. "She took me by the hand, and smiled, and said we would be friends, and that I should show her where the flowers grew; for that she had a little spot of her own that she wanted to plant with them. And she asked me if theSanguinea sanguinissima grew hereabout. I should not have taken her to be ailing in her wits, only for a kind of free-spokenness and familiarity, as if we had been acquainted a long while; or as if she had lived in some country where there are no forms and impediments in people's getting acquainted."

"Did you like her?" inquired Septimius.

"Yes; almost loved her at first sight," answered Rose, "and I hope may do her some little good, poor thing, being of her own age, and the only companion, hereabouts, whom she is likely to find. But she has been well educated, and is a lady, that is easy to see."

"It is very strange," said Septimius, "but I fear I shall be a good deal interrupted in my thoughts and studies, if she insists on haunting my hill-top as much as she tells me. My meditations are perhaps of a little too much importance to be shoved aside for the sake of gratifying a crazy girl's fantasies."

"Ah, that is a hard thing to say!" exclaimed Rose, shocked at her lover's cold egotism, though not giving it that title. "Let the poor thing glide quietly along in the path, though it be yours. Perhaps, after a while, she will help your thoughts."

"My thoughts," said Septimius, "are of a kind that can have no help from any one; if from any, it would only be from some wise, long-studied, and experienced scientific man, who could enlighten me as to the bases and foundation of things, as to mystic writings, as to chemical elements, as to the mysteries of language, as to the principles and system on which we were created. Methinks these are not to be taught me by a girl touched in the wits."

"I fear," replied Rose Garfield with gravity, and drawing imperceptibly apart from him, "that no woman can help you much. You despise woman's thought, and have no need of her affection."

Septimius said something soft and sweet, and in a measure true, in regard to the necessity he felt for the affection and sympathy of one woman at least–the one now by his side–to keep his life warm and to make the empty chambers of his heart comfortable. But even while he spoke, there was something that dragged upon his tongue; for he felt that the solitary pursuit in which he was engaged carried him apart from the sympathy of which he spoke, and that he was concentrating his efforts and interest entirely upon himself, and that the more he succeeded the more remotely he should be carried away, and that his final triumph would be the complete seclusion of himself from all that breathed,–the converting him, from an interested actor into a cold and disconnected spectator of all mankind's warm and sympathetic life. So, as it turned out, this interview with Rose was one of those in which, coming no one knows from whence, a nameless cloud springs up between two lovers, and keeps them apart from one another by a cold, sullen spell. Usually, however, it requires only one word, spoken out of the heart, to break that spell, and compel the invisible, unsympathetic medium which the enemy of love has stretched cunningly between them, to vanish, and let them come closer together than ever; but, in this case, it might be that the love was the illusive state, and the estrangement the real truth, the disenchanted verity. At all events, when the feeling passed away, in Rose's heart there was no reaction, no warmer love, as is generally the case. As for Septimius, he had other things to think about, and when he next met Rose Garfield, had forgotten that he had been sensible of a little wounded feeling, on her part, at parting.

By dint of continued poring over the manuscript, Septimius now began to comprehend that it was written in a singular mixture of Latin and ancient English, with constantly recurring paragraphs of what he was convinced was a mystic writing; and these recurring passages of complete unintelligibility seemed to be necessary to the proper understanding of any part of the document. What was discoverable was quaint, curious, but thwarting and perplexing, because it seemed to imply some very great purpose, only to be brought out by what was hidden.

Septimius had read, in the old college library during his pupilage, a work on ciphers and cryptic writing, but being drawn to it only by his curiosity respecting whatever was hidden, and not expecting ever to use his knowledge, he had obtained only the barest idea of what was necessary to the deciphering a secret passage. Judging by what he could pick out, he would have thought the whole essay was upon the moral conduct; all parts of that he could make out seeming to refer to a certain ascetic rule of life; to denial of pleasures; these topics being repeated and insisted on everywhere, although without any discoverable reference to religious or moral motives; and always when the author seemed verging towards a definite purpose, he took refuge in his cipher. Yet withal, imperfectly (or not at all, rather) as Septimius could comprehend its purport, this strange writing had a mystic influence, that wrought upon his imagination, and with the late singular incidents of his life, his continual thought on this one subject, his walk on the hill-top, lonely, or only interrupted by the pale shadow of a girl, combined to set him outside of the living world. Rose Garfield perceived it, knew and felt that he was gliding away from her, and met him with a reserve which she could not overcome.

It was a pity that his early friend, Robert Hagburn, could not at present have any influence over him, having now regularly joined the Continental Army, and being engaged in the expedition of Arnold against Quebec. Indeed, this war, in which the country was so earnestly and enthusiastically engaged, had perhaps an influence on Septimius's state of mind, for it put everybody into an exaggerated and unnatural state, united enthusiasms of all sorts, heightened everybody either into its own heroism or into the peculiar madness to which each person was inclined; and Septimius walked so much the more wildly on his lonely course, because the people were going enthusiastically on another. In times of revolution and public disturbance all absurdities are more unrestrained; the measure of calm sense, the habits, the orderly decency, are partially lost. More people become insane, I should suppose; offences against public morality, female license, are more numerous; suicides, murders, all ungovernable outbreaks of men's thoughts, embodying themselves in wild acts, take place more frequently, and with less horror to the lookers-on. So [with] Septimius; there was not, as there would have been at an ordinary time, the same calmness and truth in the public observation, scrutinizing everything with its keen criticism, in that time of seething opinions and overturned principles; a new time was coming, and Septimius's phase of novelty attracted less attention so far as it was known.

So he continued to brood over the manuscript in his study, and to hide it under lock and key in a recess of the wall, as if it were a secret of murder; to walk, too, on his hill-top, where at sunset always came the pale, crazy maiden, who still seemed to watch the little hillock with a pertinacious care that was strange to Septimius. By and by came the winter and the deep snows; and even then, unwilling to give up his habitual place of exercise, the monotonousness of which promoted his wish to keep before his mind one subject of thought, Septimius wore a path through the snow, and still walked there. Here, however, he lost for a time the companionship of the girl; for when the first snow came, she shivered, and looked at its white heap over the hillock, and said to Septimius, "I will look for it again in spring."

[Septimius is at the point of despair for want of a guide in his studies.]

67

The winter swept over, and spring was just beginning to spread its green flush over the more favored exposures of the landscape, although on the north side of stone-walls, and the northern nooks of hills, there were still the remnants of snow-drifts. Septimius's hill-top, which was of a soil which quickly rid itself of moisture, now began to be a genial place of resort to him, and he was one morning taking his walk there, meditating upon the still insurmountable difficulties which interposed themselves against the interpretation of the manuscript, yet feeling the new gush of spring bring hope to him, and the energy and elasticity for new effort. Thus pacing to and fro, he was surprised, as he turned at the extremity of his walk, to see a figure advancing towards him; not that of the pale maiden whom he was accustomed to see there, but a figure as widely different as possible. [He sees a spider dangling from his web, and examines him minutely.] It was that of a short, broad, somewhat elderly man, dressed in a surtout that had a half-military air; the cocked hat of the period, well worn, and having a fresher spot in it, whence, perhaps, a cockade had been recently taken off; and this personage carried a well blackened German pipe in his hand, which, as he walked, he applied to his lips, and puffed out volumes of smoke, filling the pleasant western breeze with the fragrance of some excellent Virginia. He came slowly along, and Septimius, slackening his pace a little, came as slowly to meet him, feeling somewhat indignant, to be sure, that anybody should intrude on his sacred hill; until at last they met, as it happened, close by the memorable little hillock, on which the grass and flower-leaves also had begun to sprout. The stranger looked keenly at Septimius, made a careless salute by putting his hand up, and took the pipe from his mouth.

"Mr. Septimius Felton, I suppose?" said he.

"That is my name," replied Septimius.

"I am Doctor Jabez Portsoaken," said the stranger, "late surgeon of his Majesty's sixteenth regiment, which I quitted when his Majesty's army quitted Boston, being desirous of trying my fortunes in your country, and giving the people the benefit of my scientific knowledge; also to practise some new modes of medical science, which I could not so well do in the army."

"I think you are quite right, Doctor Jabez Portsoaken," said Septimius, a little confused and bewildered, so unused had he become to the society of strangers.

"And as to you, sir," said the doctor, who had a very rough, abrupt way of speaking, "I have to thank you for a favor done me."

"Have you, sir?" said Septimius, who was quite sure that he had never seen the doctor's uncouth figure before.

"Oh, ay, me," said the doctor, puffing coolly,–"me in the person of my niece, a sickly, poor, nervous little thing, who is very fond of walking on your hill-top, and whom you do not send away."

"You are the uncle of Sibyl Dacy?" said Septimius.

"Even so, her mother's brother," said the doctor, with a grotesque bow. "So, being on a visit, the first that the siege allowed me to pay, to see how the girl was getting on, I take the opportunity to pay my respects to you; the more that I understand you to be a young man of some learning, and it is not often that one meets with such in this country."

"No," said Septimius, abruptly, for indeed he had half a suspicion that this queer Doctor Portsoaken was not altogether sincere,–that, in short, he was making game of him. "You have been misinformed. I know nothing whatever that is worth knowing."

"Oho!" said the doctor, with a long puff of smoke out of his pipe. "If you are convinced of that, you are one of the wisest men I have met with, young as you are. I must have been twice your age before I got so far; and even now, I am sometimes fool enough to doubt the only thing I was ever sure of knowing. But come, you make me only the more earnest to collogue with you. If we put both our shortcomings together, they may make up an item of positive knowledge."

"What use can one make of abortive thoughts?" said Septimius.

"Do your speculations take a scientific turn?" said Doctor Portsoaken. "There I can meet you with as much false knowledge and empiricism as you can bring for the life of you. Have you ever tried to study spiders?–there is my strong point now! I have hung my whole interest in life on a spider's web."

"I know nothing of them, sir," said Septimius, "except to crush them when I see them running across the floor, or to brush away the festoons of their webs when they have chanced to escape my Aunt Keziah's broom."

"Crush them! Brush away their webs!" cried the doctor, apparently in a rage, and shaking his pipe at Septimius. "Sir, it is sacrilege! Yes, it is worse than murder. Every thread of a spider's web is worth more than a thread of gold; and before twenty years are passed, a housemaid will be beaten to death with her own broomstick if she disturbs one of these sacred animals. But, come again. Shall we talk of botany, the virtues of herbs?"

"My Aunt Keziah should meet you there, doctor," said Septimius. "She has a native and original acquaintance with their virtues, and can save and kill with any of the faculty. As for myself, my studies have not turned that way."

"They ought! they ought!" said the doctor, looking meaningly at him. "The whole thing lies in the blossom of an herb. Now, you ought to begin with what lies about you; on this little hillock, for instance;" and looking at the grave beside which they were standing, he gave it a kick which went to Septimius's heart, there seemed to be such a spite and scorn in it. "On this hillock I see some specimens of plants which would be worth your looking at."

Bending down towards the grave as he spoke, he seemed to give closer attention to what he saw there; keeping in his stooping position till his face began to get a purple aspect, for the erudite doctor was of that make of man who has to be kept right side uppermost with care. At length he raised himself, muttering, "Very curious! very curious!"

"Do you see anything remarkable there?" asked Septimius, with some interest.

"Yes," said the doctor, bluntly. "No matter what! The time will come when you may like to know it."

"Will you come with me to my residence at the foot of the hill, Doctor Portsoaken?" asked Septimius. "I am not a learned man, and have little or no title to converse with one, except a sincere desire to be wiser than I am. If you can be moved on such terms to give me your companionship, I shall be thankful."

"Sir, I am with you," said Doctor Portsoaken. "I will tell you what I know, in the sure belief (for I will be frank with you) that it will add to the amount of dangerous folly now in your mind, and help you on the way to ruin. Take your choice, therefore, whether to know me further or not."

"I neither shrink nor fear,–neither hope much," said Septimius, quietly. "Anything that you can communicate–if anything you can–I shall fearlessly receive, and return you such thanks as it may be found to deserve."

So saying, he led the way down the hill, by the steep path that descended abruptly upon the rear of his bare and unadorned little dwelling; the doctor following with much foul language (for he had a terrible habit of swearing) at the difficulties of the way, to which his short legs were ill adapted. Aunt Keziah met them at the door, and looked sharply at the doctor, who returned the gaze with at least as much keenness, muttering between his teeth, as he did so; and to say the truth, Aunt Keziah was as worthy of being sworn at as any woman could well be, for whatever she might have been in her younger days, she was at this time as strange a mixture of an Indian squaw and herb doctress, with the crabbed old maid, and a mingling of the witch-aspect running through all as could well be imagined; and she had a handkerchief over her head, and she was of hue a dusky yellow, and she looked very cross. As Septimius ushered the doctor into his study, and was about to follow him, Aunt Keziah drew him back.

"Septimius, who is this you have brought here?" asked she.

"A man I have met on the hill," answered her nephew; "a Doctor Portsoaken he calls himself, from the old country. He says he has knowledge of herbs and other mysteries; in your own line, it may be. If you want to talk with him, give the man his dinner, and find out what there is in him."

"And what do you want of him yourself, Septimius?" asked she.

"I? Nothing!–that is to say, I expect nothing," said Septimius. "But I am astray, seeking everywhere, and so I reject no hint, no promise, no faintest possibility of aid that I may find anywhere. I judge this man to be a quack, but I judge the same of the most learned man of his profession, or any other; and there is a roughness about this man that may indicate a little more knowledge than if he were smoother. So, as he threw himself in my way, I take him in."

"A grim, ugly-looking old wretch as ever I saw," muttered Aunt Keziah. "Well, he shall have his dinner; and if he likes to talk about yarb-dishes, I'm with him."

So Septimius followed the doctor into his study, where he found him with the sword in his hand, which he had taken from over the mantel-piece, and was holding it drawn, examining the hilt and blade with great minuteness; the hilt being wrought in openwork, with certain heraldic devices, doubtless belonging to the family of its former wearer.

"I have seen this weapon before," said the doctor.

"It may well be," said Septimius. "It was once worn by a person who served in the army of your king."

"And you took it from him?" said the doctor.

"If I did, it was in no way that I need be ashamed of, or afraid to tell, though I choose rather not to speak of it," answered Septimius.

"Have you, then, no desire nor interest to know the family, the personal history, the prospects, of him who once wore this sword, and who will never draw sword again?" inquired Doctor Portsoaken. "Poor Cyril Norton! There was a singular story attached to that young man, sir, and a singular mystery he carried about with him, the end of which, perhaps, is not yet."

Septimius would have been, indeed, well enough pleased to learn the mystery which he himself had seen that there was about the man whom he slew; but he was afraid that some question might be thereby started about the secret document that he had kept possession of; and he therefore would have wished to avoid the whole subject.

72

"I cannot be supposed to take much interest in English family history. It is a hundred and fifty years, at least, since my own family ceased to be English," he answered. "I care more for the present and future than for the past."

"It is all one," said the doctor, sitting down, taking out a pinch of tobacco and refilling his pipe.

It is unnecessary to follow up the description of the visit of the eccentric doctor through the day. Suffice it to say that there was a sort of charm, or rather fascination, about the uncouth old fellow, in spite of his strange ways; in spite of his constant puffing of tobacco; and in spite, too, of a constant imbibing of strong liquor, which he made inquiries for, and of which the best that could be produced was a certain decoction, infusion, or distillation, pertaining to Aunt Keziah, and of which the basis was rum, be it said, done up with certain bitter herbs of the old lady's own gathering, at proper times of the moon, and which was a well-known drink to all who were favored with Aunt Keziah's friendship; though there was a story that it was the very drink which used to be passed round at witch-meetings, being brewed from the Devil's own recipe. And, in truth, judging from the taste (for I once took a sip of a draught prepared from the same ingredients, and in the same way), I should think this hellish origin might be the veritable one.

["I thought" quoth the doctor, "I could drink anything, but"–]

But the valiant doctor sipped, and sipped again, and said with great blasphemy that it was the real stuff, and only needed henbane to make it perfect. Then, taking from his pocket a good-sized leathern-covered flask, with a silver lip fastened on the muzzle, he offered it to Septimius, who declined, and to Aunt Keziah, who preferred her own decoction, and then drank it off himself, with a loud smack of satisfaction, declaring it to be infernally good brandy.

Well, after this Septimius and he talked; and I know not how it was, but there was a great deal of imagination in this queer man, whether a bodily or spiritual influence it might be hard to say. On the other hand Septimius had for a long while held little intercourse with men; none whatever with men who could comprehend him; the doctor, too, seemed to bring the discourse singularly in apposition with what his host was continually thinking about, for he conversed on occult matters, on people who had had the art of living long, and had only died at last by accident, on the powers and qualities of common herbs, which he believed to be so great, that all around our feet—growing in the wild forest, afar from man, or following the footsteps of man wherever he fixes his residence, across seas, from the old homesteads whence he migrated, following him everywhere, and offering themselves sedulously and continually to his notice, while he only plucks them away from the comparatively worthless things which he cultivates, and flings them aside, blaspheming at them because Providence has sown them so thickly—grow what we call weeds, only because all the generations, from the beginning of time till now, have failed to discover their wondrous virtues, potent for the curing of all diseases, potent for procuring length of days.

"Everything good," said the doctor, drinking another dram of brandy, "lies right at our feet, and all we need is to gather it up."

"That's true," quoth Keziah, taking just a little sup of her hellish preparation; "these herbs were all gathered within a hundred yards of this very spot, though it took a wise woman to find out their virtues."

The old woman went off about her household duties, and then it was that Septimius submitted to the doctor the list of herbs which he had picked out of the old document, asking him, as something apposite to the subject of their discourse, whether he was acquainted with them, for most of them had very queer names, some in Latin, some in English.

The bluff doctor put on his spectacles, and looked over the slip of yellow and worn paper scrutinizingly, puffing tobacco-smoke upon it in great volumes, as if thereby to make its hidden purport come out; he mumbled to himself, he took another sip from his flask; and then, putting it down on the table, appeared to meditate.

"This infernal old document," said he, at length, "is one that I have never seen before, yet heard of, nevertheless; for it was my folly in youth (and whether I am any wiser now is more than I take upon me to say, but it was my folly then) to be in quest of certain kinds of secret knowledge, which the fathers of science thought attainable. Now, in several quarters, amongst people with whom my pursuits brought me in contact, I heard of a certain recipe which had been lost for a generation or two, but which, if it could be recovered, would prove to have the true life-giving potency in it. It is said that the ancestor of a great old family in England was in possession of this secret, being a man of science, and the friend of Friar Bacon, who was said to have concocted it himself, partly from the precepts of his master, partly from his own experiments, and it is thought he might have been living to this day, if he had not unluckily been killed in the Wars of the Roses; for you know no recipe for long life would be proof against an old English arrow, or a leaden bullet from one of our own firelocks."

"And what has been the history of the thing after his death?" asked Septimius.

"It was supposed to be preserved in the family," said the doctor, "and it has always been said, that the head and eldest son of that family had it at his option to live forever, if he could only make up his mind to it. But seemingly there were difficulties in the way. There was probably a certain diet and regimen to be observed, certain strict rules of life to be kept, a certain asceticism to be imposed on the person, which was not quite agreeable to young men; and after the period of youth was passed, the human frame became incapable of being regenerated from the seeds of decay and death, which, by that time, had become strongly developed in it. In short, while young, the possessor of the secret found the terms of immortal life too hard to be accepted, since it implied the giving up of most of the things that made life desirable in his view; and when he came to a more reasonable mind, it was too late. And so, in all the generations since Friar Bacon's time, the Nortons have been born, and enjoyed their young days, and worried through their manhood, and tottered through their old age (unless taken off sooner by sword, arrow, ball, fever, or what not), and died in their beds, like men that had no such option; and so this old yellow paper has done not the least good to any mortal. Neither do I see how it can do any good to you, since you know not the rules, moral or dietetic, that are essential to its effect. But how did you come by it?"

"It matters not how," said Septimius, gloomily. "Enough that I am its rightful possessor and inheritor. Can you read these old characters?"

"Most of them," said the doctor; "but let me tell you, my young friend, I have no faith whatever in this secret; and, having meddled with such things myself, I ought to know. The old physicians and chemists had strange ideas of the virtues of plants, drugs, and minerals, and equally strange fancies as to the way of getting those virtues into action. They would throw a hundred different potencies into a caldron together, and put them on the fire, and expect to brew a potency containing all their potencies, and having a different virtue of its own. Whereas, the most likely result would be that they would counteract one another, and the concoction be of no virtue at all; or else some more powerful ingredient would tincture the whole."

He read the paper again, and continued:–

"I see nothing else so remarkable in this recipe, as that it is chiefly made up of some of the commonest things that grow; plants that you set your foot upon at your very threshold, in your garden, in your wood-walks, wherever you go. I doubt not old Aunt Keziah knows them, and very likely she has brewed them up in that hell-drink, the remembrance of which is still rankling in my stomach. I thought I had swallowed the Devil himself, whom the old woman had been boiling down. It would be curious enough if the hideous decoction was the same as old Friar Bacon and his acolyte discovered by their science! One ingredient, however, one of those plants, I scarcely think the old lady can have put into her pot of Devil's elixir; for it is a rare plant, that does not grow in these parts."

"And what is that?" asked Septimius.

"Sanguinea sanguinissima" said the doctor; "it has no vulgar name; but it produces a very beautiful flower, which I have never seen, though some seeds of it were sent me by a learned friend in Siberia. The others, divested of their Latin names, are as common as plantain, pig-weed, and burdock; and it stands to reason that, if vegetable Nature has any such wonderfully efficacious medicine in store for men, and means them to use it, she would have strewn it everywhere plentifully within their reach."

"But, after all, it would be a mockery on the old dame's part," said the young man, somewhat bitterly, "since she would thus hold the desired thing seemingly within our reach; but because she never tells us how to prepare and obtain its efficacy, we miss it just as much as if all the ingredients were hidden from sight and knowledge in the centre of the earth. We are the playthings and fools of Nature, which she amuses herself with during our little lifetime, and then breaks for mere sport, and laughs in our faces as she does so."

"Take care, my good fellow," said the doctor, with his great coarse laugh. "I rather suspect that you have already got beyond the age when the great medicine could do you good; that speech indicates a great toughness and hardness and bitterness about the heart that does not accumulate in our tender years."

Septimius took little or no notice of the raillery of the grim old doctor, but employed the rest of the time in getting as much information as he could out of his guest; and though he could not bring himself to show him the precious and sacred manuscript, yet he questioned him as closely as possible without betraying his secret, as to the modes of finding out cryptic writings. The doctor was not without the perception that his dark-browed, keen-eyed acquaintance had some purpose not openly avowed in all these pertinacious, distinct questions; he discovered a central reference in them all, and perhaps knew that Septimius must have in his possession some writing in hieroglyphics, cipher, or other secret mode, that conveyed instructions how to operate with the strange recipe that he had shown him.

"You had better trust me fully, my good sir," said he. "Not but what I will give you all the aid I can without it; for you have done me a greater benefit than you are aware of, beforehand. No—you will not? Well, if you can change your mind, seek me out in Boston, where I have seen fit to settle in the practice of my profession, and I will serve you according to your folly; for folly it is, I warn you."

Nothing else worthy of record is known to have passed during the doctor's visit; and in due time he disappeared, as it were, in a whiff of tobacco-smoke, leaving an odor of brandy and tobacco behind him, and a traditionary memory of a wizard that had been there. Septimius went to work with what items of knowledge he had gathered from him; but the interview had at least made him aware of one thing, which was, that he must provide himself with all possible quantity of scientific knowledge of botany, and perhaps more extensive knowledge, in order to be able to concoct the recipe. It was the fruit of all the scientific attainment of the age that produced it (so said the legend, which seemed reasonable enough), a great philosopher had wrought his learning into it; and this had been attempered, regulated, improved, by the quick, bright intellect of his scholar. Perhaps, thought Septimius, another deep and earnest intelligence added to these two may bring the precious recipe to still greater perfection. At least it shall be tried. So thinking, he gathered together all the books that he could find relating to such studies; he spent one day, moreover, in a walk to Cambridge, where he searched the alcoves of the college library for such works as it contained; and borrowing them from the war-disturbed institution of learning, he betook himself homewards, and applied himself to the study with an earnestness of zealous application that perhaps has been seldom equalled in a study of so quiet a character. A month or two of study, with practice upon such plants as he found upon his hill-top, and along the brook and in other neighboring localities, sufficed to do a great deal for him. In this pursuit he was assisted by Sibyl, who proved to have great knowledge in some botanical departments, especially among flowers; and in her cold and quiet way, she met him on this subject and glided by his side, as she had done so long, a companion, a daily observer and observed of him, mixing herself up with his pursuits, as if she were an attendant sprite upon him.

But this pale girl was not the only associate of his studies, the only instructress, whom Septimius found. The observation which Doctor Portsoaken made about the fantastic possibility that Aunt Keziah might have inherited the same recipe from her Indian ancestry which had been struck out by the science of Friar Bacon and his pupil had not failed to impress Septimius, and to remain on his memory. So, not long after the doctor's departure, the young man took occasion one evening to say to his aunt that he thought his stomach was a little out of order with too much application, and that perhaps she could give him some herb-drink or other that would be good for him.

"That I can, Seppy, my darling," said the old woman, "and I'm glad you have the sense to ask for it at last. Here it is in this bottle; and though that foolish, blaspheming doctor turned up his old brandy nose at it, I'll drink with him any day and come off better than he."

So saying, she took out of the closet her brown jug, stopped with a cork that had a rag twisted round it to make it tighter, filled a mug half full of the concoction and set it on the table before Septimius.

"There, child, smell of that; the smell merely will do you good; but drink it down, and you'll live the longer for it."

"Indeed, Aunt Keziah, is that so?" asked Septimius, a little startled by a recommendation which in some measure tallied with what he wanted in a medicine. "That's a good quality."

He looked into the mug, and saw a turbid, yellow concoction, not at all attractive to the eye; he smelt of it, and was partly of opinion that Aunt Keziah had mixed a certain unfragrant vegetable, called skunk-cabbage, with the other ingredients of her witch-drink. He tasted it; not a mere sip, but a good, genuine gulp, being determined to have real proof of what the stuff was in all respects. The draught seemed at first to burn in his mouth, unaccustomed to any drink but water, and to go scorching all the way down into his stomach, making him sensible of the depth of his inwards by a track of fire, far, far down; and then, worse than the fire, came a taste of hideous bitterness and nauseousness, which he had not previously conceived to exist, and which threatened to stir up his bowels into utter revolt; but knowing Aunt Keziah's touchiness with regard to this concoction, and how sacred she held it, he made an effort of real heroism, squelched down his agony, and kept his face quiet, with the exception of one strong convulsion, which he allowed to twist across it for the sake of saving his life.

"It tastes as if it might have great potency in it, Aunt Keziah," said this unfortunate young man. "I wish you would tell me what it is made of, and how you brew it; for I have observed you are very strict and secret about it."

"Aha! you have seen that, have you?" said Aunt Keziah, taking a sip of her beloved liquid, and grinning at him with a face and eyes as yellow as that she was drinking. In fact the idea struck him, that in temper, and all appreciable qualities, Aunt Keziah was a good deal like this drink of hers, having probably become saturated by them while she drank of it. And then, having drunk, she gloated over it, and tasted, and smelt of the cup of this hellish wine, as a winebibber does of that which is most fragrant and delicate. "And you want to know how I make it? But first, child, tell me honestly, do you love this drink of mine? Otherwise, here, and at once, we stop talking about it."

"I love it for its virtues," said Septimius, temporizing with his conscience, "and would prefer it on that account to the rarest wines."

"So far good," said Aunt Keziah, who could not well conceive that her liquor should be otherwise than delicious to the palate. "It is the most virtuous liquor that ever was; and therefore one need not fear drinking too much of it. And you want to know what it is made of? Well; I have often thought of telling you, Seppy, my boy, when you should come to be old enough; for I have no other inheritance to leave you, and you are all of my blood, unless I should happen to have some far-off uncle among the Cape Indians. But first, you must know how this good drink, and the faculty of making it, came down to me from the chiefs, and sachems, and Peow-wows, that were your ancestors and mine, Septimius, and from the old wizard who was my great-grandfather and yours, and who, they say, added the fire-water to the other ingredients, and so gave it the only one thing that it wanted to make it perfect."

And so Aunt Keziah, who had now put herself into a most comfortable and jolly state by sipping again, and after pressing Septimius to mind his draught (who declined, on the plea that one dram at a time was enough for a new beginner, its virtues being so strong, as well as admirable), the old woman told him a legend strangely wild and uncouth, and mixed up of savage and civilized life, and of the superstitions of both, but which yet had a certain analogy, that impressed Septimius much, to the story that the doctor had told him.

80

She said that, many ages ago, there had been a wild sachem in the forest, a king among the Indians, and from whom, the old lady said, with a look of pride, she and Septimius were lineally descended, and were probably the very last who inherited one drop of that royal, wise, and warlike blood. The sachem had lived very long, longer than anybody knew, for the Indians kept no record, and could only talk of a great number of moons; and they said he was as old, or older, than the oldest trees; as old as the hills almost, and could remember back to the days of godlike men, who had arts then forgotten. He was a wise and good man, and could foretell as far into the future as he could remember into the past; and he continued to live on, till his people were afraid that he would live forever, and so disturb the whole order of nature; and they thought it time that so good a man, and so great a warrior and wizard, should be gone to the happy hunting-grounds, and that so wise a counsellor should go and tell his experience of life to the Great Father, and give him an account of matters here, and perhaps lead him to make some changes in the conduct of the lower world. And so, all these things duly considered, they very reverently assassinated the great, never-dying sachem; for though safe against disease, and undecayable by age, he was capable of being killed by violence, though the hardness of his skull broke to fragments the stone tomahawk with which they at first tried to kill him.

So a deputation of the best and bravest of the tribe went to the great sachem, and told him their thought, and reverently desired his consent to be put out of the world; and the undying one agreed with them that it was better for his own comfort that he should die, and that he had long been weary of the world, having learned all that it could teach him, and having, chiefly, learned to despair of ever making the red race much better than they now were. So he cheerfully consented, and told them to kill him if they could; and first they tried the stone hatchet, which was broken against his skull; and then they shot arrows at him, which could not pierce the toughness of his skin; and finally they plastered up his nose and mouth (which kept uttering wisdom to the last) with clay, and set him to bake in the sun; so at last his life burnt out of his breast, tearing his body to pieces, and he died.

81

[Make this legend grotesque, and express the weariness of the tribe at the intolerable control the undying one had of them; his always bringing up precepts from his own experience, never consenting to anything new, and so impeding progress; his habits hardening into him, his ascribing to himself all wisdom, and depriving everybody of his right to successive command; his endless talk, and dwelling on the past, so that the world could not bear him. Describe his ascetic and severe habits, his rigid calmness, etc.]

But before the great sagamore died he imparted to a chosen one of his tribe, the next wisest to himself, the secret of a potent and delicious drink, the constant imbibing of which, together with his abstinence from luxury and passion, had kept him alive so long, and would doubtless have compelled him to live forever. This drink was compounded of many ingredients, all of which were remembered and handed down in tradition, save one, which, either because it was nowhere to be found, or for some other reason, was forgotten; so that the drink ceased to give immortal life as before. They say it was a beautiful purple flower. [Perhaps the Devil taught him the drink, or else the Great Spirit,–doubtful which.] But it still was a most excellent drink, and conducive to health, and the cure of all diseases; and the Indians had it at the time of the settlement by the English; and at one of those wizard meetings in the forest, where the Black Man used to meet his red children and his white ones, and be jolly with them, a great Indian wizard taught the secret to Septimius's great-grandfather, who was a wizard, and died for it; and he, in return, taught the Indians to mix it with rum, thinking that this might be the very ingredient that was missing, and that by adding it he might give endless life to himself and all his Indian friends, among whom he had taken a wife.

"But your great-grandfather, you know, had not a fair chance to test its virtues, having been hanged for a wizard; and as for the Indians, they probably mixed too much fire-water with their liquid, so that it burnt them up, and they all died; and my mother, and her mother,–who taught the drink to me,–and her mother afore her, thought it a sin to try to live longer than the Lord pleased, so they let themselves die. And though the drink is good, Septimius, and toothsome, as you see, yet I sometimes feel as if I were getting old, like other people, and may die in the course of the next half-century;

so perhaps the rum was not just the thing that was wanting to make up the recipe. But it is very good! Take a drop more of it, dear."

"Not at present, I thank you, Aunt Keziah," said Septimius, gravely; "but will you tell me what the ingredients are, and how you make it?"

"Yes, I will, my boy, and you shall write them down," said the old woman; "for it's a good drink, and none the worse, it may be, for not making you live forever. I sometimes think I had as lief go to heaven as keep on living here."

Accordingly, making Septimius take pen and ink, she proceeded to tell him a list of plants and herbs, and forest productions, and he was surprised to find that it agreed most wonderfully with the recipe contained in the old manuscript, as he had puzzled it out, and as it had been explained by the doctor. There were a few variations, it is true; but even here there was a close analogy, plants indigenous to America being substituted for cognate productions, the growth of Europe. Then there was another difference in the mode of preparation, Aunt Keziah's nostrum being a concoction, whereas the old manuscript gave a process of distillation. This similarity had a strong effect on Septimius's imagination. Here was, in one case, a drink suggested, as might be supposed, to a primitive people by something similar to that instinct by which the brute creation recognizes the medicaments suited to its needs, so that they mixed up fragrant herbs for reasons wiser than they knew, and made them into a salutary potion; and here, again, was a drink contrived by the utmost skill of a great civilized philosopher, searching the whole field of science for his purpose; and these two drinks proved, in all essential particulars, to be identically the same.

"O Aunt Keziah," said he, with a longing earnestness, "are you sure that you cannot remember that one ingredient?"

"No, Septimius, I cannot possibly do it," said she. "I have tried many things, skunk-cabbage, wormwood, and a thousand things; for it is truly a pity that the chief benefit of the thing should be lost for so little. But the only effect was, to spoil the good taste of the stuff, and, two or three times, to poison myself, so that I broke out all over blotches, and once lost the use of my left arm, and got a dizziness in the head, and a rheumatic twist in my knee, a hardness of hearing, and a dimness of sight, and the trembles; all of which I certainly believe to have been caused by my putting something else into this blessed drink besides the good New England rum. Stick to that, Seppy, my dear."

So saying, Aunt Keziah took yet another sip of the beloved liquid, after vainly pressing Septimius to do the like; and then lighting her old clay pipe, she sat down in the chimney-corner, meditating, dreaming, muttering pious prayers and ejaculations, and sometimes looking up the wide flue of the chimney, with thoughts, perhaps, how delightful it must have been to fly up there, in old times, on excursions by midnight into the forest, where was the Black Man, and the Puritan deacons and ladies, and those wild Indian ancestors of hers; and where the wildness of the forest was so grim and delightful, and so unlike the common-placeness in which she spent her life. For thus did the savage strain of the woman, mixed up as it was with the other weird and religious parts of her composition, sometimes snatch her back into barbarian life and its instincts; and in Septimius, though further diluted, and modified likewise by higher cultivation, there was the same tendency.

Septimius escaped from the old woman, and was glad to breathe the free air again; so much had he been wrought upon by her wild legends and wild character, the more powerful by its analogy with his own; and perhaps, too, his brain had been a little bewildered by the draught of her diabolical concoction which she had compelled him to take. At any rate, he was glad to escape to his hill-top, the free air of which had doubtless contributed to keep him in health through so long a course of morbid thought and estranged study as he had addicted himself to.

Here, as it happened, he found both Rose Garfield and Sibyl Dacy, whom the pleasant summer evening had brought out. They had formed a friendship, or at least society; and there could not well be a pair more unlike,– the one so natural, so healthy, so fit to live in the world; the other such a morbid, pale thing. So there they were, walking arm in arm, with one arm round each other's waist, as girls love to do. They greeted the young man in their several ways, and began to walk to and fro together, looking at the sunset as it came on, and talking of things on earth and in the clouds.

"When has Robert Hagburn been heard from?" asked Septimius, who, involved in his own pursuits, was altogether behindhand in the matters of the war,–shame to him for it!

"There came news, two days past," said Rose, blushing. "He is on his way home with the remnant of General Arnold's command, and will be here soon."

"He is a brave fellow, Robert," said Septimius, carelessly. "And I know not, since life is so short, that anything better can be done with it than to risk it as he does."

"I truly think not," said Rose Garfield, composedly.

"What a blessing it is to mortals," said Sibyl Dacy, "what a kindness of Providence, that life is made so uncertain; that death is thrown in among the possibilities of our being; that these awful mysteries are thrown around us, into which we may vanish! For, without it, how would it be possible to be heroic, how should we plod along in commonplaces forever, never dreaming high things, never risking anything? For my part, I think man is more favored than the angels, and made capable of higher heroism, greater virtue, and of a more excellent spirit than they, because we have such a mystery of grief and terror around us; whereas they, being in a certainty of God's light, seeing his goodness and his purposes more perfectly than we, cannot be so brave as often poor weak man, and weaker woman, has the opportunity to be, and sometimes makes use of it. God gave the whole world to man, and if he is left alone with it, it will make a clod of him at last; but, to remedy that, God gave man a grave, and it redeems all, while it seems to destroy all, and makes an immortal spirit of him in the end."

"Dear Sibyl, you are inspired," said Rose, gazing in her face.

"I think you ascribe a great deal too much potency to the grave," said Septimius, pausing involuntarily alone by the little hillock, whose contents he knew so well. "The grave seems to me a vile pitfall, put right in our pathway, and catching most of us,–all of us,–causing us to tumble in at the most inconvenient opportunities, so that all human life is a jest and a farce, just for the sake of this inopportune death; for I observe it never waits for us to accomplish anything: we may have the salvation of a country in hand, but we are none the less likely to die for that. So that, being a believer, on the whole, in the wisdom and graciousness of Providence, I am convinced that dying is a mistake, and that by and by we shall overcome it. I say there is no use in the grave."

"I still adhere to what I said," answered Sibyl Dacy; "and besides, there is another use of a grave which I have often observed in old English graveyards, where the moss grows green, and embosses the letters of the gravestones; and also graves are very good for flower-beds."

Nobody ever could tell when the strange girl was going to say what was laughable,—when what was melancholy; and neither of Sibyl's auditors knew quite what to make of this speech. Neither could Septimius fail to be a little startled by seeing her, as she spoke of the grave as a flower-bed, stoop down to the little hillock to examine the flowers, which, indeed, seemed to prove her words by growing there in strange abundance, and of many sorts; so that, if they could all have bloomed at once, the spot would have looked like a bouquet by itself, or as if the earth were richest in beauty there, or as if seeds had been lavished by some florist. Septimius could not account for it, for though the hill-side did produce certain flowers,—the aster, the golden-rod, the violet, and other such simple and common things,—yet this seemed as if a carpet of bright colors had been thrown down there and covered the spot.

"This is very strange," said he.

"Yes," said Sibyl Dacy, "there is some strange richness in this little spot of soil."

"Where could the seeds have come from?—that is the greatest wonder," said Rose. "You might almost teach me botany, methinks, on this one spot."

"Do you know this plant?" asked Sibyl of Septimius, pointing to one not yet in flower, but of singular leaf, that was thrusting itself up out of the ground, on the very centre of the grave, over where the breast of the sleeper below might seem to be. "I think there is no other here like it."

Septimius stooped down to examine it, and was convinced that it was unlike anything he had seen of the flower kind; a leaf of a dark green, with purple veins traversing it, it had a sort of questionable aspect, as some plants have, so that you would think it very likely to be poison, and would not like to touch or smell very intimately, without first inquiring who would be its guarantee that it should do no mischief. That it had some richness or other, either baneful or beneficial, you could not doubt.

"I think it poisonous," said Rose Garfield, shuddering, for she was a person so natural she hated poisonous things, or anything speckled especially, and did not, indeed, love strangeness. "Yet I should not wonder if it bore a beautiful flower by and by. Nevertheless, if I were to do just as I feel inclined, I should root it up and fling it away."

"Shall she do so?" said Sibyl to Septimius.

"Not for the world," said he, hastily. "Above all things, I desire to see what will come of this plant."

"Be it as you please," said Sibyl. "Meanwhile, if you like to sit down here and listen to me, I will tell you a story that happens to come into my mind just now,—I cannot tell why. It is a legend of an old hall that I know well, and have known from my childhood, in one of the northern counties of England, where I was born. Would you like to hear it, Rose?"

"Yes, of all things," said she. "I like all stories of hall and cottage in the old country, though now we must not call it our country any more."

Sibyl looked at Septimius, as if to inquire whether he, too, chose to listen to her story, and he made answer:—

"Yes, I shall like to hear the legend, if it is a genuine one that has been adopted into the popular belief, and came down in chimney-corners with the smoke and soot that gathers there; and incrusted over with humanity, by passing from one homely mind to another. Then, such stories get to be true, in a certain sense, and indeed in that sense may be called true throughout, for the very nucleus, the fiction in them, seems to have come out of the heart of man in a way that cannot be imitated of malice aforethought. Nobody can make a tradition; it takes a century to make it."

"I know not whether this legend has the character you mean," said Sibyl, "but it has lived much more than a century; and here it is.

"On the threshold of one of the doors of —— Hall there is a bloody footstep impressed into the doorstep, and ruddy as if the bloody foot had just trodden there; and it is averred that, on a certain night of the year, and at a certain hour of the night, if you go and look at that doorstep you will see the mark wet with fresh blood. Some have pretended to say that this appearance of blood was but dew; but can dew redden a cambric handkerchief? Will it crimson the fingertips when you touch it? And that is what the bloody footstep will surely do when the appointed night and hour come round, this very year, just as it would three hundred years ago.

"Well; but how did it come there? I know not precisely in what age it was, but long ago, when light was beginning to shine into what were called the dark ages, there was a lord of —— Hall who applied himself deeply to knowledge and science, under the guidance of the wisest man of that age,–a man so wise that he was thought to be a wizard; and, indeed, he may have been one, if to be a wizard consists in having command over secret powers of nature, that other men do not even suspect the existence of, and the control of which enables one to do feats that seem as wonderful as raising the dead. It is needless to tell you all the strange stories that have survived to this day about the old Hall; and how it is believed that the master of it, owing to his ancient science, has still a sort of residence there, and control of the place; and how, in one of the chambers, there is still his antique table, and his chair, and some rude old instruments and machinery, and a book, and everything in readiness, just as if he might still come back to finish some experiment. What it is important to say is, that one of the chief things to which the old lord applied himself was to discover the means of prolonging his own life, so that its duration should be indefinite, if not infinite; and such was his science, that he was believed to have attained this magnificent and awful purpose.

"So, as you may suppose, the man of science had great joy in having done this thing, both for the pride of it, and because it was so delightful a thing to have before him the prospect of endless time, which he might spend in adding more and more to his science, and so doing good to the world; for the chief obstruction to the improvement of the world and the growth of knowledge is, that mankind cannot go straightforward in it, but continually there have to be new beginnings, and it takes every new man half his life, if not the whole of it, to come up to the point where his predecessor left off. And so this noble man–this man of a noble purpose–spent many years in finding out this mighty secret; and at last, it is said, he succeeded. But on what terms?

"Well, it is said that the terms were dreadful and horrible; insomuch that the wise man hesitated whether it were lawful and desirable to take advantage of them, great as was the object in view.

"You see, the object of the lord of —— Hall was to take a life from the course of Nature, and Nature did not choose to be defrauded; so that, great as was the power of this scientific man over her, she would not consent that he should escape the necessity of dying at his proper time, except upon condition of sacrificing some other life for his; and this was to be done once for every thirty years that he chose to live, thirty years being the account of a generation of man; and if in any way, in that time, this lord could be the death of a human being, that satisfied the requisition, and he might live on. There is a form of the legend which says, that one of the ingredients of the drink which the nobleman brewed by his science was the heart's blood of a pure young boy or girl. But this I reject, as too coarse an idea; and, indeed, I think it may be taken to mean symbolically, that the person who desires to engross to himself more than his share of human life must do it by sacrificing to his selfishness some dearest interest of another person, who has a good right to life, and may be as useful in it as he.

"Now, this lord was a just man by nature, and if he had gone astray, it was greatly by reason of his earnest wish to do something for the poor, wicked, struggling, bloody, uncomfortable race of man, to which he belonged. He bethought himself whether he would have a right to take the life of one of those creatures, without their own consent, in order to prolong his own; and after much arguing to and fro, he came to the conclusion that he should not have the right, unless it were a life over which he had control, and which was the next to his own. He looked round him; he was a lonely and abstracted man, secluded by his studies from human affections, and there was but one human being whom he cared for;–that was a beautiful kinswoman, an orphan, whom his father had brought up, and, dying, left her to his care. There was great kindness and affection–as great as the abstracted nature of his pursuits would allow–on the part of this lord towards the beautiful young girl; but not what is called love,–at least, he never acknowledged it to himself. But, looking into his heart, he saw that she, if any one, was to be the person whom the sacrifice demanded, and that he might kill twenty others without effect, but if he took the life of this one, it would make the charm strong and good.

"My friends, I have meditated many a time on this ugly feature of my legend, and am unwilling to take it in the literal sense; so I conceive its spiritual meaning (for everything, you know, has its spiritual meaning, which to the literal meaning is what the soul is to the body),–its spiritual meaning was, that to the deep pursuit of science we must sacrifice great part of the joy of life; that nobody can be great, and do great things, without giving up to death, so far as he regards his enjoyment of it, much that he would gladly enjoy; and in that sense I choose to take it. But the earthly old legend will have it that this mad, high-minded, heroic, murderous lord did insist upon it with himself that he must murder this poor, loving, and beloved child.

"I do not wish to delay upon this horrible matter, and to tell you how he argued it with himself; and how, the more and more he argued it, the more reasonable it seemed, the more absolutely necessary, the more a duty that the terrible sacrifice should be made. Here was this great good to be done to mankind, and all that stood in the way of it was one little delicate life, so frail that it was likely enough to be blown out, any day, by the mere rude blast that the rush of life creates, as it streams along, or by any slightest accident; so good and pure, too, that she was quite unfit for this world, and not capable of any happiness in it; and all that was asked of her was to allow herself to be transported to a place where she would be happy, and would find companions fit for her,–which he, her only present companion, certainly was not. In fine, he resolved to shed the sweet, fragrant blood of this little violet that loved him so.

"Well; let us hurry over this part of the story as fast as we can. He did slay this pure young girl; he took her into the wood near the house, an old wood that is standing yet, with some of its magnificent oaks; and then he plunged a dagger into her heart, after they had had a very tender and loving talk together, in which he had tried to open the matter tenderly to her, and make her understand that, though he was to slay her, it was really for the very reason that he loved her better than anything else in the world, and that he would far rather die himself, if that would answer the purpose at all. Indeed, he is said to have offered her the alternative of slaying him, and taking upon herself the burden of indefinite life, and the studies and pursuits by which he meant to benefit mankind. But she, it is said,—this noble, pure, loving child,—she looked up into his face and smiled sadly, and then snatching the dagger from him, she plunged it into her own heart. I cannot tell whether this be true, or whether she waited to be killed by him; but this I know, that in the same circumstances I think I should have saved my lover or my friend the pain of killing me. There she lay dead, at any rate, and he buried her in the wood, and returned to the house; and, as it happened, he had set his right foot in her blood, and his shoe was wet in it, and by some miraculous fate it left a track all along the wood-path, and into the house, and on the stone steps of the threshold, and up into his chamber, all along; and the servants saw it the next day, and wondered, and whispered, and missed the fair young girl, and looked askance at their lord's right foot, and turned pale, all of them, as death.

"And next, the legend says, that Sir Forrester was struck with horror at what he had done, and could not bear the laboratory where he had toiled so long, and was sick to death of the object that he had pursued, and was most miserable, and fled from his old Hall, and was gone full many a day. But all the while he was gone there was the mark of a bloody footstep impressed upon the stone doorstep of the Hall. The track had lain all along through the wood-path, and across the lawn, to the old Gothic door of the Hall; but the rain, the English rain, that is always falling, had come the next day, and washed it all away. The track had lain, too, across the broad hall, and up the stairs, and into the lord's study; but there it had lain on the rushes that were strewn there, and these the servants had gathered carefully up, and thrown them away, and spread fresh ones. So that it was only on the threshold that the mark remained.

"But the legend says, that wherever Sir Forrester went, in his wanderings about the world, he left a bloody track behind him. It was wonderful, and very inconvenient, this phenomenon. When he went into a church, you would see the track up the broad aisle, and a little red puddle in the place where he sat or knelt. Once he went to the king's court, and there being a track up to the very throne, the king frowned upon him, so that he never came there any more. Nobody could tell how it happened; his foot was not seen to bleed, only there was the bloody track behind him, wherever he went; and he was a horror-stricken man, always looking behind him to see the track, and then hurrying onward, as if to escape his own tracks; but always they followed him as fast.

"In the hall of feasting, there was the bloody track to his chair. The learned men whom he consulted about this strange difficulty conferred with one another, and with him, who was equal to any of them, and pished and pshawed, and said, 'Oh, there is nothing miraculous in this; it is only a natural infirmity, which can easily be put an end to, though, perhaps, the stoppage of such an evacuation will cause damage to other parts of the frame.' Sir Forrester always said, 'Stop it, my learned brethren, if you can; no matter what the consequences.' And they did their best, but without result; so that he was still compelled to leave his bloody track on their college-rooms and combination-rooms, the same as elsewhere; and in street and in wilderness; yes, and in the battle-field, they said, his track looked freshest and reddest of all. So, at last, finding the notice he attracted inconvenient, this unfortunate lord deemed it best to go back to his own Hall, where, living among faithful old servants born in the family, he could hush the matter up better than elsewhere, and not be stared at continually, or, glancing round, see people holding up their hands in terror at seeing a bloody track behind him. And so home he came, and there he saw the bloody track on the doorstep, and dolefully went into the hall, and up the stairs, an old servant ushering him into his chamber, and half a dozen others following behind, gazing, shuddering, pointing with quivering fingers, looking horror-stricken in one another's pale faces, and the moment he had passed, running to get fresh rushes, and to scour the stairs. The next day, Sir Forrester went into the wood, and by the aged oak he found a grave, and on the grave he beheld a beautiful crimson flower; the most gorgeous and beautiful, surely, that ever grew; so rich it looked, so full of potent juice.

That flower he gathered; and the spirit of his scientific pursuits coming upon him, he knew that this was the flower, produced out of a human life, that was essential to the perfection of his recipe for immortality; and he made the drink, and drank it, and became immortal in woe and agony, still studying, still growing wiser and more wretched in every age. By and by he vanished from the old Hall, but not by death; for, from generation to generation, they say that a bloody track is seen around that house, and sometimes it is tracked up into the chambers, so freshly that you see he must have passed a short time before; and he grows wiser and wiser, and lonelier and lonelier, from age to age. And this is the legend of the bloody footstep, which I myself have seen at the Hall door. As to the flower, the plant of it continued for several years to grow out of the grave; and after a while, perhaps a century ago, it was transplanted into the garden of —— Hall, and preserved with great care, and is so still. And as the family attribute a kind of sacredness, or cursedness, to the flower, they can hardly be prevailed upon to give any of the seeds, or allow it to be propagated elsewhere, though the king should send to ask it. It is said, too, that there is still in the family the old lord's recipe for immortality, and that several of his collateral descendants have tried to concoct it, and instil the flower into it, and so give indefinite life; but unsuccessfully, because the seeds of the flower must be planted in a fresh grave of bloody death, in order to make it effectual."

So ended Sibyl's legend; in which Septimius was struck by a certain analogy to Aunt Keziah's Indian legend,–both referring to a flower growing out of a grave; and also he did not fail to be impressed with the wild coincidence of this disappearance of an ancestor of the family long ago, and the appearance, at about the same epoch, of the first known ancestor of his own family, the man with wizard's attributes, with the bloody footstep, and whose sudden disappearance became a myth, under the idea that the Devil carried him away. Yet, on the whole, this wild tradition, doubtless becoming wilder in Sibyl's wayward and morbid fancy, had the effect to give him a sense of the fantasticalness of his present pursuit, and that in adopting it, he had strayed into a region long abandoned to superstition, and where the shadows of forgotten dreams go when men are done with them; where past worships are; where great Pan went when he died to the outer world; a limbo into which living men sometimes stray when they think themselves sensiblest and wisest, and whence they do not often find their way back into the real world. Visions of wealth, visions of fame, visions of philanthropy,—all visions find room here, and glide about without jostling. When Septimius came to look at the matter in his present mood, the thought occurred to him that he had perhaps got into such a limbo, and that Sibyl's legend, which looked so wild, might be all of a piece with his own present life; for Sibyl herself seemed an illusion, and so, most strangely, did Aunt Keziah, whom he had known all his life, with her homely and quaint characteristics; the grim doctor, with his brandy and his German pipe, impressed him in the same way; and these, altogether, made his homely cottage by the wayside seem an unsubstantial edifice, such as castles in the air are built of, and the ground he trod on unreal; and that grave, which he knew to contain the decay of a beautiful young man, but a fictitious swell, formed by the fantasy of his eyes. All unreal; all illusion! Was Rose Garfield a deception too, with her daily beauty, and daily cheerfulness, and daily worth? In short, it was such a moment as I suppose all men feel (at least, I can answer for one), when the real scene and picture of life swims, jars, shakes, seems about to be broken up and dispersed, like the picture in a smooth pond, when we disturb its tranquil mirror by throwing in a stone; and though the scene soon settles itself, and looks as real as before, a haunting doubt keeps close at hand, as long as we live, asking, "Is it stable? Am I sure of it? Am I certainly not dreaming? See; it trembles again, ready to dissolve."

Applying himself with earnest diligence to his attempt to decipher and interpret the mysterious manuscript, working with his whole mind and strength, Septimius did not fail of some flattering degree of success.

A good deal of the manuscript, as has been said, was in an ancient English script, although so uncouth and shapeless were the characters, that it was not easy to resolve them into letters, or to believe that they were anything but arbitrary and dismal blots and scrawls upon the yellow paper; without meaning, vague, like the misty and undefined germs of thought as they exist in our minds before clothing themselves in words. These, however, as he concentrated his mind upon them, took distincter shape, like cloudy stars at the power of the telescope, and became sometimes English, sometimes Latin, strangely patched together, as if, so accustomed was the writer to use that language in which all the science of that age was usually embodied, that he really mixed it unconsciously with the vernacular, or used both indiscriminately. There was some Greek, too, but not much. Then frequently came in the cipher, to the study of which Septimius had applied himself for some time back, with the aid of the books borrowed from the college library, and not without success. Indeed, it appeared to him, on close observation, that it had not been the intention of the writer really to conceal what he had written from any earnest student, but rather to lock it up for safety in a sort of coffer, of which diligence and insight should be the key, and the keen intelligence with which the meaning was sought should be the test of the seeker's being entitled to possess the secret treasure.

Amid a great deal of misty stuff, he found the document to consist chiefly, contrary to his supposition beforehand, of certain rules of life; he would have taken it, on a casual inspection, for an essay of counsel, addressed by some great and sagacious man to a youth in whom he felt an interest,—so secure and good a doctrine of life was propounded, such excellent maxims there were, such wisdom in all matters that came within the writer's purview. It was as much like a digested synopsis of some old philosopher's wise rules of conduct, as anything else. But on closer inspection, Septimius, in his unsophisticated consideration of this matter, was not so well satisfied. True, everything that was said seemed not discordant with the rules of social morality; not unwise: it was shrewd, sagacious; it did not appear to infringe upon the rights of mankind; but there was something left out, something unsatisfactory,—what was it? There was certainly a cold spell in the document; a magic, not of fire, but of ice; and Septimius the more exemplified its power, in that he soon began to be insensible of it. It affected him as if it had been written by some greatly wise and worldly-experienced man, like the writer of Ecclesiastes; for it was full of truth. It was a truth that does not make men better, though perhaps calmer; and beneath which the buds of happiness curl up like tender leaves in a frost. What was the matter with this document, that the young man's youth perished out of him as he read? What icy hand had written, it, so that the heart was chilled out of the reader? Not that Septimius was sensible of this character; at least, not long,–for as he read, there grew upon him a mood of calm satisfaction, such as he had never felt before. His mind seemed to grow clearer; his perceptions most acute; his sense of the reality of things grew to be such, that he felt as if he could touch and handle all his thoughts, feel round about all their outline and circumference, and know them with a certainty, as if they were material things. Not that all this was in the document itself; but by studying it so earnestly, and, as it were, creating its meaning anew for himself, out of such illegible materials, he caught the temper of the old writer's mind, after so many ages as that tract had lain in the mouldy and musty manuscript. He was magnetized with him; a powerful intellect acted powerfully upon him; perhaps, even, there was a sort of spell and mystic influence imbued into the paper, and mingled with the yellow ink, that steamed forth by the effort of this young man's earnest rubbing, as it were, and by the action of his mind, applied to it as intently as he possibly could; and even his handling the paper, his bending over it, and breathing upon it, had its effect.

It is not in our power, nor in our wish, to produce the original form, nor yet the spirit, of a production which is better lost to the world: because it was the expression of a human intellect originally greatly gifted and capable of high things, but gone utterly astray, partly by its own subtlety, partly by yielding to the temptations of the lower part of its nature, by yielding the spiritual to a keen sagacity of lower things, until it was quite fallen; and yet fallen in such a way, that it seemed not only to itself, but to mankind, not fallen at all, but wise and good, and fulfilling all the ends of intellect in such a life as ours, and proving, moreover, that earthly life was good, and all that the development of our nature demanded. All this is better forgotten; better burnt; better never thought over again; and all the more, because its aspect was so wise, and even praiseworthy. But what we must preserve of it were certain rules of life and moral diet, not exactly expressed in the document, but which, as it were, on its being duly received into Septimius's mind, were precipitated from the rich solution, and crystallized into diamonds, and which he found to be the moral dietetics, so to speak, by observing which he was to achieve the end of earthly immortality, whose physical nostrum was given in the recipe which, with the help of Doctor Portsoaken and his Aunt Keziah, he had already pretty satisfactorily made out.

"Keep thy heart at seventy throbs in a minute; all more than that wears away life too quickly. If thy respiration be too quick, think with thyself that thou hast sinned against natural order and moderation.

"Drink not wine nor strong drink; and observe that this rule is worthiest in its symbolic meaning.

"Bask daily in the sunshine and let it rest on thy heart.

"Run not; leap not; walk at a steady pace, and count thy paces per day.

"If thou feelest, at any time, a throb of the heart, pause on the instant, and analyze it; fix thy mental eye steadfastly upon it, and inquire why such commotion is.

"Hate not any man nor woman; be not angry, unless at any time thy blood seem a little cold and torpid; cut out all rankling feelings, they are poisonous to thee. If, in thy waking moments, or in thy dreams, thou hast thoughts of strife or unpleasantness with any man, strive quietly with thyself to forget him.

"Have no friendships with an imperfect man, with a man in bad health, of violent passions, of any characteristic that evidently disturbs his own life, and so may have disturbing influence on thine. Shake not any man by the hand, because thereby, if there be any evil in the man, it is likely to be communicated to thee.

"Kiss no woman if her lips be red; look not upon her if she be very fair. Touch not her hand if thy finger-tips be found to thrill with hers ever so little. On the whole, shun woman, for she is apt to be a disturbing influence. If thou love her, all is over, and thy whole past and remaining labor and pains will be in vain.

"Do some decent degree of good and kindness in thy daily life, for the result is a slight pleasurable sense that will seem to warm and delectate thee with felicitous self-laudings; and all that brings thy thoughts to thyself tends to invigorate that central principle by the growth of which thou art to give thyself indefinite life.

"Do not any act manifestly evil; it may grow upon thee, and corrode thee in after-years. Do not any foolish good act; it may change thy wise habits.

"Eat no spiced meats. Young chickens, new-fallen lambs, fruits, bread four days old, milk, freshest butter will make thy fleshy tabernacle youthful.

"From sick people, maimed wretches, afflicted people–all of whom show themselves at variance with things as they should be,–from people beyond their wits, from people in a melancholic mood, from people in extravagant joy, from teething children, from dead corpses, turn away thine eyes and depart elsewhere.

"If beggars haunt thee, let thy servants drive them away, thou withdrawing out of ear-shot.

"Crying and sickly children, and teething children, as aforesaid, carefully avoid. Drink the breath of wholesome infants as often as thou conveniently canst,–it is good for thy purpose; also the breath of buxom maids, if thou mayest without undue disturbance of the flesh, drink it as a morning-draught, as medicine; also the breath of cows as they return from rich pasture at eventide.

"If thou seest human poverty, or suffering, and it trouble thee, strive moderately to relieve it, seeing that thus thy mood will be changed to a pleasant self-laudation.

"Practise thyself in a certain continual smile, for its tendency will be to compose thy frame of being, and keep thee from too much wear.

"Search not to see if thou hast a gray hair; scrutinize not thy forehead to find a wrinkle; nor the corners of thy eyes to discover if they be corrugated. Such things, being gazed at, daily take heart and grow.

"Desire nothing too fervently, not even life; yet keep thy hold upon it mightily, quietly, unshakably, for as long as thou really art resolved to live, Death with all his force, shall have no power against thee.

"Walk not beneath tottering ruins, nor houses being put up, nor climb to the top of a mast, nor approach the edge of a precipice, nor stand in the way of the lightning, nor cross a swollen river, nor voyage at sea, nor ride a skittish horse, nor be shot at by an arrow, nor confront a sword, nor put thyself in the way of violent death; for this is hateful, and breaketh through all wise rules.

"Say thy prayers at bedtime, if thou deemest it will give thee quieter sleep; yet let it not trouble thee if thou forgettest them.

"Change thy shirt daily; thereby thou castest off yesterday's decay, and imbibest the freshness of the morning's life, which enjoy with smelling to roses, and other healthy and fragrant flowers, and live the longer for it. Roses are made to that end.

"Read not great poets; they stir up thy heart; and the human heart is a soil which, if deeply stirred, is apt to give out noxious vapors."

Such were some of the precepts which Septimius gathered and reduced to definite form out of this wonderful document; and he appreciated their wisdom, and saw clearly that they must be absolutely essential to the success of the medicine with which they were connected. In themselves, almost, they seemed capable of prolonging life to an indefinite period, so wisely were they conceived, so well did they apply to the causes which almost invariably wear away this poor short life of men, years and years before even the shattered constitutions that they received from their forefathers need compel them to die. He deemed himself well rewarded for all his labor and pains, should nothing else follow but his reception and proper appreciation of these wise rules; but continually, as he read the manuscript, more truths, and, for aught I know, profounder and more practical ones, developed themselves; and, indeed, small as the manuscript looked, Septimius thought that he should find a volume as big as the most ponderous folio in the college library too small to contain its wisdom. It seemed to drip and distil with precious fragrant drops, whenever he took it out of his desk; it diffused wisdom like those vials of perfume which, small as they look, keep diffusing an airy wealth of fragrance for years and years together, scattering their virtue in incalculable volumes of invisible vapor, and yet are none the less in bulk for all they give; whenever he turned over the yellow leaves, bits of gold, diamonds of good size, precious pearls, seemed to drop out from between them.

And now ensued a surprise which, though of a happy kind, was almost too much for him to bear; for it made his heart beat considerably faster than the wise rules of his manuscript prescribed. Going up on his hill-top, as summer wore away (he had not been there for some time), and walking by the little flowery hillock, as so many a hundred times before, what should he see there but a new flower, that during the time he had been poring over the manuscript so sedulously had developed itself, blossomed, put forth its petals, bloomed into full perfection, and now, with the dew of the morning upon it, was waiting to offer itself to Septimius? He trembled as he looked at it, it was too much almost to bear,–it was so very beautiful, so very stately, so very rich, so very mysterious and wonderful. It was like a person, like a life! Whence did it come? He stood apart from it, gazing in wonder; tremulously taking in its aspect, and thinking of the legends he had heard from Aunt Keziah and from Sibyl Dacy; and how that this flower, like the one that their wild traditions told of, had grown out of a grave,–out of a grave in which he had laid one slain by himself.

The flower was of the richest crimson, illuminated with a golden centre of a perfect and stately beauty. From the best descriptions that I have been able to gain of it, it was more like a dahlia than any other flower with which I have acquaintance; yet it does not satisfy me to believe it really of that species, for the dahlia is not a flower of any deep characteristics, either lively or malignant, and this flower, which Septimius found so strangely, seems to have had one or the other. If I have rightly understood, it had a fragrance which the dahlia lacks; and there was something hidden in its centre, a mystery, even in its fullest bloom, not developing itself so openly as the heartless, yet not dishonest, dahlia. I remember in England to have seen a flower at Eaton Hall, in Cheshire, in those magnificent gardens, which may have been like this, but my remembrance of it is not sufficiently distinct to enable me to describe it better than by saying that it was crimson, with a gleam of gold in its centre, which yet was partly hidden. It had many petals of great richness.

Septimius, bending eagerly over the plant, saw that this was not to be the only flower that it would produce that season; on the contrary, there was to be a great abundance of them, a luxuriant harvest; as if the crimson offspring of this one plant would cover the whole hillock,—as if the dead youth beneath had burst into a resurrection of many crimson flowers! And in its veiled heart, moreover, there was a mystery like death, although it seemed to cover something bright and golden.

Day after day the strange crimson flower bloomed more and more abundantly, until it seemed almost to cover the little hillock, which became a mere bed of it, apparently turning all its capacity of production to this flower; for the other plants, Septimius thought, seemed to shrink away, and give place to it, as if they were unworthy to compare with the richness, glory, and worth of this their queen. The fervent summer burned into it, the dew and the rain ministered to it; the soil was rich, for it was a human heart contributing its juices,—a heart in its fiery youth sodden in its own blood, so that passion, unsatisfied loves and longings, ambition that never won its object, tender dreams and throbs, angers, lusts, hates, all concentrated by life, came sprouting in it, and its mysterious being, and streaks and shadows, had some meaning in each of them.

The two girls, when they next ascended the hill, saw the strange flower, and Rose admired it, and wondered at it, but stood at a distance, without showing an attraction towards it, rather an undefined aversion, as if she thought it might be a poison flower; at any rate she would not be inclined to wear it in her bosom. Sibyl Dacy examined it closely, touched its leaves, smelt it, looked at it with a botanist's eye, and at last remarked to Rose, "Yes, it grows well in this new soil; methinks it looks like a new human life."

"What is the strange flower?" asked Rose.

"The Sanguinea sanguinissima" said Sibyl.

It so happened about this time that poor Aunt Keziah, in spite of her constant use of that bitter mixture of hers, was in a very bad state of health. She looked all of an unpleasant yellow, with bloodshot eyes; she complained terribly of her inwards. She had an ugly rheumatic hitch in her motion from place to place, and was heard to mutter many wishes that she had a broomstick to fly about upon, and she used to bind up her head with a dishclout, or what looked to be such, and would sit by the kitchen fire even in the warm days, bent over it, crouching as if she wanted to take the whole fire into her poor cold heart or gizzard,–groaning regularly with each breath a spiteful and resentful groan, as if she fought womanfully with her infirmities; and she continually smoked her pipe, and sent out the breath of her complaint visibly in that evil odor; and sometimes she murmured a little prayer, but somehow or other the evil and bitterness, acridity, pepperiness, of her natural disposition overcame the acquired grace which compelled her to pray, insomuch that, after all, you would have thought the poor old woman was cursing with all her rheumatic might. All the time an old, broken-nosed, brown earthen jug, covered with the lid of a black teapot, stood on the edge of the embers, steaming forever, and sometimes bubbling a little, and giving a great puff, as if it were sighing and groaning in sympathy with poor Aunt Keziah, and when it sighed there came a great steam of herby fragrance, not particularly pleasant, into the kitchen. And ever and anon,–half a dozen times it might be,–of an afternoon, Aunt Keziah took a certain bottle from a private receptacle of hers, and also a teacup, and likewise a little, old-fashioned silver teaspoon, with which she measured three teaspoonfuls of some spirituous liquor into the teacup, half filled the cup with the hot decoction, drank it off, gave a grunt of content, and for the space of half an hour appeared to find life tolerable.

But one day poor Aunt Keziah found herself unable, partly from rheumatism, partly from other sickness or weakness, and partly from dolorous ill-spirits, to keep about any longer, so she betook herself to her bed; and betimes in the forenoon Septimius heard a tremendous knocking on the floor of her bedchamber, which happened to be the room above his own. He was the only person in or about the house; so with great reluctance, he left his studies, which were upon the recipe, in respect to which he was trying to make out the mode of concoction, which was told in such a mysterious way that he could not well tell either the quantity of the ingredients, the mode of trituration, nor in what way their virtue was to be extracted and combined.

Running hastily up stairs, he found Aunt Keziah lying in bed, and groaning with great spite and bitterness; so that, indeed, it seemed not improvidential that such an inimical state of mind towards the human race was accompanied with an almost inability of motion, else it would not be safe to be within a considerable distance of her.

"Seppy, you good-for-nothing, are you going to see me lying here, dying, without trying to do anything for me?"

"Dying, Aunt Keziah?" repeated the young man. "I hope not! What can I do for you? Shall I go for Rose? or call a neighbor in? or the doctor?"

"No, no, you fool!" said the afflicted person. "You can do all that anybody can for me; and that is to put my mixture on the kitchen fire till it steams, and is just ready to bubble; then measure three teaspoonfuls–or it may be four, as I am very bad–of spirit into a teacup, fill it half full,–or it may be quite full, for I am very bad, as I said afore; six teaspoonfuls of spirit into a cup of mixture, and let me have it as soon as may be; and don't break the cup, nor spill the precious mixture, for goodness knows when I can go into the woods to gather any more. Ah me! ah me! it's a wicked, miserable world, and I am the most miserable creature in it. Be quick, you good-for-nothing, and do as I say!"

Septimius hastened down; but as he went a thought came into his head, which it occurred to him might result in great benefit to Aunt Keziah, as well as to the great cause of science and human good, and to the promotion of his own purpose, in the first place. A day or two ago, he had gathered several of the beautiful flowers, and laid them in the fervid sun to dry; and they now seemed to be in about the state in which the old woman was accustomed to use her herbs, so far as Septimius had observed. Now if these flowers were really, as there was so much reason for supposing, the one ingredient that had for hundreds of years been missing out of Aunt Keziah's nostrum,–if it was this which that strange Indian sagamore had mingled with his drink with such beneficial effect,–why should not Septimius now restore it, and if it would not make his beloved aunt young again, at least assuage the violent symptoms, and perhaps prolong her valuable life some years, for the solace and delight of her numerous friends? Septimius, like other people of investigating and active minds, had a great tendency to experiment, and so good an opportunity as the present, where (perhaps he thought) there was so little to be risked at worst, and so much to be gained, was not to be neglected; so, without more ado, he stirred three of the crimson flowers into the earthen jug, set it on the edge of the fire, stirred it well, and when it steamed, threw up little scarlet bubbles, and was about to boil, he measured out the spirits, as Aunt Keziah had bidden him and then filled the teacup.

"Ah, this will do her good; little does she think, poor old thing, what a rare and costly medicine is about to be given her. This will set her on her feet again."

The hue was somewhat changed, he thought, from what he had observed of Aunt Keziah's customary decoction; instead of a turbid yellow, the crimson petals of the flower had tinged it, and made it almost red; not a brilliant red, however, nor the least inviting in appearance. Septimius smelt it, and thought he could distinguish a little of the rich odor of the flower, but was not sure. He considered whether to taste it; but the horrible flavor of Aunt Keziah's decoction recurred strongly to his remembrance, and he concluded that were he evidently at the point of death, he might possibly be bold enough to taste it again; but that nothing short of the hope of a century's existence at least would repay another taste of that fierce and nauseous bitterness. Aunt Keziah loved it; and as she brewed, so let her drink.

He went up stairs, careful not to spill a drop of the brimming cup, and approached the old woman's bedside, where she lay, groaning as before, and breaking out into a spiteful croak the moment he was within ear-shot.

"You don't care whether I live or die," said she. "You've been waiting in hopes I shall die, and so save yourself further trouble."

"By no means, Aunt Keziah," said Septimius. "Here is the medicine, which I have warmed, and measured out, and mingled, as well as I knew how; and I think it will do you a great deal of good."

"Won't you taste it, Seppy, my dear?" said Aunt Keziah, mollified by the praise of her beloved mixture. "Drink first, dear, so that my sick old lips need not taint it. You look pale, Septimius; it will do you good."

"No, Aunt Keziah, I do not need it; and it were a pity to waste your precious drink," said he.

"It does not look quite the right color," said Aunt Keziah, as she took the cup in her hand. "You must have dropped some soot into it." Then, as she raised it to her lips, "It does not smell quite right. But, woe's me! how can I expect anybody but myself to make this precious drink as it should be?"

She drank it off at two gulps; for she appeared to hurry it off faster than usual, as if not tempted by the exquisiteness of its flavor to dwell upon it so long.

"You have not made it just right, Seppy," said she in a milder tone than before, for she seemed to feel the customary soothing influence of the draught, "but you'll do better the next time. It had a queer taste, methought; or is it that my mouth is getting out of taste? Hard times it will be for poor Aunt Kezzy, if she's to lose her taste for the medicine that, under Providence, has saved her life for so many years."

She gave back the cup to Septimius, after looking a little curiously at the dregs.

"It looks like bloodroot, don't it?" said she. "Perhaps it's my own fault after all. I gathered a fresh bunch of the yarbs yesterday afternoon, and put them to steep, and it may be I was a little blind, for it was between daylight and dark, and the moon shone on me before I had finished. I thought how the witches used to gather their poisonous stuff at such times, and what pleasant uses they made of it,–but those are sinful thoughts, Seppy, sinful thoughts! so I'll say a prayer and try to go to sleep. I feel very noddy all at once."

Septimius drew the bedclothes up about her shoulders, for she complained of being very chilly, and, carefully putting her stick within reach, went down to his own room, and resumed his studies, trying to make out from those aged hieroglyphics, to which he was now so well accustomed, what was the precise method of making the elixir of immortality. Sometimes, as men in deep thought do, he rose from his chair, and walked to and fro the four or five steps or so that conveyed him from end to end of his little room. At one of these times he chanced to look in the little looking-glass that hung between the windows, and was startled at the paleness of his face. It was quite white, indeed. Septimius was not in the least a foppish young man; careless he was in dress, though often his apparel took an unsought picturesqueness that set off his slender, agile figure, perhaps from some quality of spontaneous arrangement that he had inherited from his Indian ancestry. Yet many women might have found a charm in that dark, thoughtful face, with its hidden fire and energy, although Septimius never thought of its being handsome, and seldom looked at it. Yet now he was drawn to it by seeing how strangely white it was, and, gazing at it, he observed that since he considered it last, a very deep furrow, or corrugation, or fissure, it might almost be called, had indented his brow, rising from the commencement of his nose towards the centre of the forehead. And he knew it was his brooding thought, his fierce, hard determination, his intense concentrativeness for so many months, that had been digging that furrow; and it must prove indeed a potent specific of the life-water that would smooth that away, and restore him all the youth and elasticity that he had buried in that profound grave.

But why was he so pale? He could have supposed himself startled by some ghastly thing that he had just seen; by a corpse in the next room, for instance; or else by the foreboding that one would soon be there; but yet he was conscious of no tremor in his frame, no terror in his heart; as why should there be any? Feeling his own pulse, he found the strong, regular beat that should be there. He was not ill, nor affrighted; not expectant of any pain. Then why so ghastly pale? And why, moreover, Septimius, did you listen so earnestly for any sound in Aunt Keziah's chamber? Why did you creep on tiptoe, once, twice, three times, up to the old woman's chamber, and put your ear to the keyhole, and listen breathlessly? Well; it must have been that he was subconscious that he was trying a bold experiment, and that he had taken this poor old woman to be the medium of it, in the hope, of course, that it would turn out well; yet with other views than her interest in the matter. What was the harm of that? Medical men, no doubt, are always doing so, and he was a medical man for the time. Then why was he so pale?

He sat down and fell into a reverie, which perhaps was partly suggested by that chief furrow which he had seen, and which we have spoken of, in his brow. He considered whether there was anything in this pursuit of his that used up life particularly fast; so that, perhaps, unless he were successful soon, he should be incapable of renewal; for, looking within himself, and considering his mode of being, he had a singular fancy that his heart was gradually drying up, and that he must continue to get some moisture for it, or else it would soon be like a withered leaf. Supposing his pursuit were vain, what a waste he was making of that little treasure of golden days, which was his all! Could this be called life, which he was leading now? How unlike that of other young men! How unlike that of Robert Hagburn, for example! There had come news yesterday of his having performed a gallant part in the battle of Monmouth, and being promoted to be a captain for his brave conduct. Without thinking of long life, he really lived in heroic actions and emotions; he got much life in a little, and did not fear to sacrifice a lifetime of torpid breaths, if necessary, to the ecstasy of a glorious death!

[It appears from a written sketch by the author of this story, that he changed his first plan of making Septimius and Rose lovers, and she was to be represented as his half-sister, and in the copy for publication this alteration would have been made.—ED.]

And then Robert loved, too, loved his sister Rose, and felt, doubtless, an immortality in that passion. Why could not Septimius love too? It was forbidden! Well, no matter; whom could he have loved? Who, in all this world would have been suited to his secret, brooding heart, that he could have let her into its mysterious chambers, and walked with her from one cavernous gloom to another, and said, "Here are my treasures. I make thee mistress of all these; with all these goods I thee endow." And then, revealing to her his great secret and purpose of gaining immortal life, have said: "This shall be thine, too. Thou shalt share with me. We will walk along the endless path together, and keep one another's hearts warm, and so be content to live."

Ah, Septimius! but now you are getting beyond those rules of yours, which, cold as they are, have been drawn out of a subtle philosophy, and might, were it possible to follow them out, suffice to do all that you ask of them; but if you break them, you do it at the peril of your earthly immortality. Each warmer and quicker throb of the heart wears away so much of life. The passions, the affections, are a wine not to be indulged in. Love, above all, being in its essence an immortal thing, cannot be long contained in an earthly body, but would wear it out with its own secret power, softly invigorating as it seems. You must be cold, therefore, Septimius; you must not even earnestly and passionately desire this immortality that seems so necessary to you. Else the very wish will prevent the possibility of its fulfilment.

By and by, to call him out of these rhapsodies, came Rose home; and finding the kitchen hearth cold, and Aunt Keziah missing, and no dinner by the fire, which was smouldering,–nothing but the portentous earthen jug, which fumed, and sent out long, ill-flavored sighs, she tapped at Septimius's door, and asked him what was the matter.

"Aunt Keziah has had an ill turn," said Septimius, "and has gone to bed."

"Poor auntie!" said Rose, with her quick sympathy. "I will this moment run up and see if she needs anything."

"No, Rose," said Septimius, "she has doubtless gone to sleep, and will awake as well as usual. It would displease her much were you to miss your afternoon school; so you had better set the table with whatever there is left of yesterday's dinner, and leave me to take care of auntie."

"Well," said Rose, "she loves you best; but if she be really ill, I shall give up my school and nurse her."

"No doubt," said Septimius, "she will be about the house again to-morrow."

So Rose ate her frugal dinner (consisting chiefly of purslain, and some other garden herbs, which her thrifty aunt had prepared for boiling), and went away as usual to her school; for Aunt Keziah, as aforesaid, had never encouraged the tender ministrations of Rose, whose orderly, womanly character, with its well-defined orb of daily and civilized duties, had always appeared to strike her as tame; and she once said to her, "You are no squaw, child, and you'll never make a witch." Nor would she even so much as let

Rose put her tea to steep, or do anything whatever for herself personally; though, certainly, she was not backward in requiring of her a due share of labor for the general housekeeping.

Septimius was sitting in his room, as the afternoon wore away; because, for some reason or other, or, quite as likely, for no reason at all, he did not air himself and his thoughts, as usual, on the hill; so he was sitting musing, thinking, looking into his mysterious manuscript, when he heard Aunt Keziah moving in the chamber above. First she seemed to rattle a chair; then she began a slow, regular beat with the stick which Septimius had left by her bedside, and which startled him strangely,–so that, indeed, his heart beat faster than the five-and-seventy throbs to which he was restricted by the wise rules that he had digested. So he ran hastily up stairs, and behold, Aunt Keziah was sitting up in bed, looking very wild,–so wild that you would have thought she was going to fly up chimney the next minute; her gray hair all dishevelled, her eyes staring, her hands clutching forward, while she gave a sort of howl, what with pain and agitation.

"Seppy! Seppy!" said she,–"Seppy, my darling! are you quite sure you remember how to make that precious drink?"

"Quite well, Aunt Keziah," said Septimius, inwardly much alarmed by her aspect, but preserving a true Indian composure of outward mien. "I wrote it down, and could say it by heart besides. Shall I make you a fresh pot of it? for I have thrown away the other."

"That was well, Seppy," said the poor old woman, "for there is something wrong about it; but I want no more, for, Seppy dear, I am going fast out of this world, where you and that precious drink were my only treasures and comforts. I wanted to know if you remembered the recipe; it is all I have to leave you, and the more you drink of it, Seppy, the better. Only see to make it right!"

"Dear auntie, what can I do for you?" said Septimius, in much consternation, but still calm. "Let me run for the doctor,–for the neighbors? something must be done!"

The old woman contorted herself as if there were a fearful time in her insides; and grinned, and twisted the yellow ugliness of her face, and groaned, and howled; and yet there was a tough and fierce kind of endurance with which she fought with her anguish, and would not yield to it a jot, though she allowed herself the relief of shrieking savagely at it,–much more like a defiance than a cry for mercy.

"No doctor! no woman!" said she; "if my drink could not save me, what would a doctor's foolish pills and powders do? And a woman! If old Martha Denton, the witch, were alive, I would be glad to see her. But other women! Pah! Ah! Ai! Oh! Phew! Ah, Seppy, what a mercy it would be now if I could set to and blaspheme a bit, and shake my fist at the sky! But I'm a Christian woman, Seppy,–a Christian woman."

"Shall I send for the minister, Aunt Keziah?" asked Septimius. "He is a good man, and a wise one."

"No minister for me, Seppy," said Aunt Keziah, howling as if somebody were choking her. "He may be a good man, and a wise one, but he's not wise enough to know the way to my heart, and never a man as was! Eh, Seppy, I'm a Christian woman, but I'm not like other Christian women; and I'm glad I'm going away from this stupid world. I've not been a bad woman, and I deserve credit for it, for it would have suited me a great deal better to be bad. Oh, what a delightful time a witch must have had, starting off up chimney on her broomstick at midnight, and looking down from aloft in the sky on the sleeping village far below, with its steeple pointing up at her, so that she might touch the golden weathercock! You, meanwhile, in such an ecstasy, and all below you the dull, innocent, sober humankind; the wife sleeping by her husband, or mother by her child, squalling with wind in its stomach; the goodman driving up his cattle and his plough,–all so innocent, all so stupid, with their dull days just alike, one after another. And you up in the air, sweeping away to some nook in the forest! Ha! What's that? A wizard! Ha! ha! Known below as a deacon! There is Goody Chickering! How quietly she sent the young people to bed after prayers! There is an Indian; there a nigger; they all have equal rights and privileges at a witch-meeting. Phew! the wind blows cold up here! Why does not the Black Man have the meeting at his own kitchen hearth? Ho! ho! Oh dear me! But I'm a Christian woman and no witch; but those must have been gallant times!"

Doubtless it was a partial wandering of the mind that took the poor old woman away on this old-witch flight; and it was very curious and pitiful to witness the compunction with which she returned to herself and took herself to task for the preference which, in her wild nature, she could not help giving to harum-scarum wickedness over tame goodness. Now she tried to compose herself, and talk reasonably and godly.

"Ah, Septimius, my dear child, never give way to temptation, nor consent to be a wizard, though the Black Man persuade you ever so hard. I know he will try. He has tempted me, but I never yielded, never gave him his will; and never do you, my boy, though you, with your dark complexion, and your brooding brow, and your eye veiled, only when it suddenly looks out with a flash of fire in it, are the sort of man he seeks most, and that afterwards serves him. But don't do it, Septimius. But if you could be an Indian, methinks it would be better than this tame life we lead. 'T would have been better for me, at all events. Oh, how pleasant 't would have been to spend my life wandering in the woods, smelling the pines and the hemlock all day, and fresh things of all kinds, and no kitchen work to do,–not to rake up the fire, nor sweep the room, nor make the beds,–but to sleep on fresh boughs in a wigwam, with the leaves still on the branches that made the roof! And then to see the deer brought in by the red hunter, and the blood streaming from the arrow-dart! Ah! and the fight too! and the scalping! and, perhaps, a woman might creep into the battle, and steal the wounded enemy away of her tribe and scalp him, and be praised for it! O Seppy, how I hate the thought of the dull life women lead! A white woman's life is so dull! Thank Heaven, I'm done with it! If I'm ever to live again, may I be whole Indian, please my Maker!"

After this goodly outburst, Aunt Keziah lay quietly for a few moments, and her skinny claws being clasped together, and her yellow visage grinning, as pious an aspect as was attainable by her harsh and pain-distorted features, Septimius perceived that she was in prayer. And so it proved by what followed, for the old woman turned to him with a grim tenderness on her face, and stretched out her hand to be taken in his own. He clasped the bony talon in both his hands.

"Seppy, my dear, I feel a great peace, and I don't think there is so very much to trouble me in the other world. It won't be all house-work, and keeping decent, and doing like other people there. I suppose I needn't expect to ride on a broomstick,–that would be wrong in any kind of a world,–but there may be woods to wander in, and a pipe to smoke in the air of heaven; trees to hear the wind in, and to smell of, and all such natural, happy things; and by and by I shall hope to see you there, Seppy, my darling boy! Come by and by; 't is n't worth your while to live forever, even if you should find out what's wanting in the drink I've taught you. I can see a little way into the next world now, and I see it to be far better than this heavy and wretched old place. You'll die when your time comes; won't you, Seppy, my darling?"

"Yes, dear auntie, when my time comes," said Septimius. "Very likely I shall want to live no longer by that time."

"Likely not," said the old woman. "I'm sure I don't. It is like going to sleep on my mother's breast to die. So good night, dear Seppy!"

"Good night, and God bless you, auntie!" said Septimius, with a gush of tears blinding him, spite of his Indian nature.

The old woman composed herself, and lay quite still and decorous for a short time; then, rousing herself a little, "Septimius," said she, "is there just a little drop of my drink left? Not that I want to live any longer, but if I could sip ever so little, I feel as if I should step into the other world quite cheery, with it warm in my heart, and not feel shy and bashful at going among strangers."

"Not one drop, auntie."

"Ah, well, no matter! It was not quite right, that last cup. It had a queer taste. What could you have put into it, Seppy, darling? But no matter, no matter! It's a precious stuff, if you make it right. Don't forget the herbs, Septimius. Something wrong had certainly got into it."

These, except for some murmurings, some groanings and unintelligible whisperings, were the last utterances of poor Aunt Keziah, who did not live a great while longer, and at last passed away in a great sigh, like a gust of wind among the trees, she having just before stretched out her hand again and grasped that of Septimius; and he sat watching her and gazing at her, wondering and horrified, touched, shocked by death, of which he had so unusual a terror,–and by the death of this creature especially, with whom he felt a sympathy that did not exist with any other person now living. So long did he sit, holding her hand, that at last he was conscious that it was growing cold within his own, and that the stiffening fingers clutched him, as if they were disposed to keep their hold, and not forego the tie that had been so peculiar.

Then rushing hastily forth, he told the nearest available neighbor, who was Robert Hagburn's mother; and she summoned some of her gossips, and came to the house, and took poor Aunt Keziah in charge. They talked of her with no great respect, I fear, nor much sorrow, nor sense that the community would suffer any great deprivation in her loss; for, in their view, she was a dram-drinking, pipe-smoking, cross-grained old maid, and, as some thought, a witch; and, at any rate, with too much of the Indian blood in her to be of much use; and they hoped that now Rose Garfield would have a pleasanter life, and Septimius study to be a minister, and all things go well, and the place be cheerfuller. They found Aunt Keziah's bottle in the cupboard, and tasted and smelt of it.

"Good West Indjy as ever I tasted," said Mrs. Hagburn; "and there stands her broken pitcher, on the hearth. Ah, empty! I never could bring my mind to taste it; but now I'm sorry I never did, for I suppose nobody in the world can make any more of it."

Septimius, meanwhile, had betaken himself to the hill-top, which was his place of refuge on all occasions when the house seemed too stifled to contain him; and there he walked to and fro, with a certain kind of calmness and indifference that he wondered at; for there is hardly anything in this world so strange as the quiet surface that spreads over a man's mind in his greatest emergencies: so that he deems himself perfectly quiet, and upbraids himself with not feeling anything, when indeed he is passion-stirred. As Septimius walked to and fro, he looked at the rich crimson flowers, which seemed to be blooming in greater profusion and luxuriance than ever before. He had made an experiment with these flowers, and he was curious to know whether that experiment had been the cause of Aunt Keziah's death. Not that he felt any remorse therefor, in any case, or believed himself to have committed a crime, having really intended and desired nothing but good. I suppose such things (and he must be a lucky physician, methinks, who has no such mischief within his own experience) never weigh with deadly weight on any man's conscience. Something must be risked in the cause of science, and in desperate cases something must be risked for the patient's self. Septimius, much as he loved life, would not have hesitated to put his own life to the same risk that he had imposed on Aunt Keziah; or, if he did hesitate, it would have been only because, if the experiment turned out disastrously in his own person, he would not be in a position to make another and more successful trial; whereas, by trying it on others, the man of science still reserves himself for new efforts, and does not put all the hopes of the world, so far as involved in his success, on one cast of the die.

By and by he met Sibyl Dacy, who had ascended the hill, as was usual with her, at sunset, and came towards him, gazing earnestly in his face.

"They tell me poor Aunt Keziah is no more," said she.

"She is dead," said Septimius.

"The flower is a very famous medicine," said the girl, "but everything depends on its being applied in the proper way."

"Do you know the way, then?" asked Septimius.

"No; you should ask Doctor Portsoaken about that," said Sibyl.

Doctor Portsoaken! And so he should consult him. That eminent chemist and scientific man had evidently heard of the recipe, and at all events would be acquainted with the best methods of getting the virtues out of flowers and herbs, some of which, Septimius had read enough to know, were poison in one phase and shape of preparation, and possessed of richest virtues in others; their poison, as one may say, serving as a dark and terrible safeguard, which Providence has set to watch over their preciousness; even as a dragon, or some wild and fiendish spectre, is set to watch and keep hidden gold and heaped-up diamonds. A dragon always waits on everything that is very good. And what would deserve the watch and ward of danger of a dragon, or something more fatal than a dragon, if not this treasure of which Septimius was in quest, and the discovery and possession of which would enable him to break down one of the strongest barriers of nature? It ought to be death, he acknowledged it, to attempt such a thing; for how hanged would be life if he should succeed; how necessary it was that mankind should be defended from such attempts on the general rule on the part of all but him. How could Death be spared?– then the sire would live forever, and the heir never come to his inheritance, and so he would at once hate his own father, from the perception that he would never be out of his way. Then the same class of powerful minds would always rule the state, and there would never be a change of policy. [Here several pages are missing.–ED.]

Through such scenes Septimius sought out the direction that Doctor Portsoaken had given him, and came to the door of a house in the olden part of the town. The Boston of those days had very much the aspect of provincial towns in England, such as may still be seen there, while our own city has undergone such wonderful changes that little likeness to what our ancestors made it can now be found. The streets, crooked and narrow; the houses, many gabled, projecting, with latticed windows and diamond panes; without sidewalks; with rough pavements.

Septimius knocked loudly at the door, nor had long to wait before a serving-maid appeared, who seemed to be of English nativity; and in reply to his request for Doctor Portsoaken bade him come in, and led him up a staircase with broad landing-places; then tapped at the door of a room, and was responded to by a gruff voice saying, "Come in!" The woman held the door open, and Septimius saw the veritable Doctor Portsoaken in an old, faded morning-gown, and with a nightcap on his head, his German pipe in his mouth, and a brandy-bottle, to the best of our belief, on the table by his side.

"Come in, come in," said the gruff doctor, nodding to Septimius. "I remember you. Come in, man, and tell me your business."

Septimius did come in, but was so struck by the aspect of Dr. Portsoaken's apartment, and his gown, that he did not immediately tell his business. In the first place, everything looked very dusty and dirty, so that evidently no woman had ever been admitted into this sanctity of a place; a fact made all the more evident by the abundance of spiders, who had spun their webs about the walls and ceiling in the wildest apparent confusion, though doubtless each individual spider knew the cordage which he had lengthened out of his own miraculous bowels. But it was really strange. They had festooned their cordage on whatever was stationary in the room, making a sort of gray, dusky tapestry, that waved portentously in the breeze, and flapped, heavy and dismal, each with its spider in the centre of his own system. And what was most marvellous was a spider over the doctor's head; a spider, I think, of some South American breed, with a circumference of its many legs as big, unless I am misinformed, as a teacup, and with a body in the midst as large as a dollar; giving the spectator horrible qualms as to what would be the consequence if this spider should be crushed, and, at the same time, suggesting the poisonous danger of suffering such a monster to live. The monster, however, sat in the midst of the stalwart cordage of his web, right over the doctor's head; and he looked, with all those complicated lines, like the symbol of a conjurer or crafty politician in the midst of the complexity of his scheme; and Septimius wondered if he were not the type of Dr. Portsoaken himself, who, fat and bloated as the spider, seemed to be the centre of some dark contrivance. And could it be that poor Septimius was typified by the fascinated fly, doomed to be entangled by the web?

"Good day to you," said the gruff doctor, taking his pipe from his mouth. "Here I am, with my brother spiders, in the midst of my web. I told you, you remember, the wonderful efficacy which I had discovered in spiders' webs; and this is my laboratory, where I have hundreds of workmen concocting my panacea for me. Is it not a lovely sight?"

"A wonderful one, at least," said Septimius. "That one above your head, the monster, is calculated to give a very favorable idea of your theory. What a quantity of poison there must be in him!"

"Poison, do you call it?" quoth the grim doctor. "That's entirely as it may be used. Doubtless his bite would send a man to kingdom come; but, on the other hand, no one need want a better life-line than that fellow's web. He and I are firm friends, and I believe he would know my enemies by instinct. But come, sit down, and take a glass of brandy. No? Well, I'll drink it for you. And how is the old aunt yonder, with her infernal nostrum, the bitterness and nauseousness of which my poor stomach has not yet forgotten?"

"My Aunt Keziah is no more," said Septimius.

"No more! Well, I trust in Heaven she has carried her secret with her," said the doctor. "If anything could comfort you for her loss, it would be that. But what brings you to Boston?"

"Only a dried flower or two," said Septimius, producing some specimens of the strange growth of the grave. "I want you to tell me about them."

The naturalist took the flowers in his hand, one of which had the root appended, and examined them with great minuteness and some surprise; two or three times looking in Septimius's face with a puzzled and inquiring air; then examined them again.

"Do you tell me," said he, "that the plant has been found indigenous in this country, and in your part of it? And in what locality?"

"Indigenous, so far as I know," answered Septimius. "As to the locality,"– he hesitated a little,–"it is on a small hillock, scarcely bigger than a molehill, on the hill-top behind my house."

The naturalist looked steadfastly at him with red, burning eyes, under his deep, impending, shaggy brows; then again at the flower.

"Flower, do you call it?" said he, after a reëxamination. "This is no flower, though it so closely resembles one, and a beautiful one,–yes, most beautiful. But it is no flower. It is a certain very rare fungus,–so rare as almost to be thought fabulous; and there are the strangest superstitions, coming down from ancient times, as to the mode of production. What sort of manure had been put into that hillock? Was it merely dried leaves, the refuse of the forest, or something else?"

Septimius hesitated a little; but there was no reason why he should not disclose the truth,—as much of it as Doctor Portsoaken cared to know.

"The hillock where it grew," answered he, "was a grave."

"A grave! Strange! strange!" quoth Doctor Portsoaken. "Now these old superstitions sometimes prove to have a germ of truth in them, which some philosopher has doubtless long ago, in forgotten ages, discovered and made known; but in process of time his learned memory passes away, but the truth, undiscovered, survives him, and the people get hold of it, and make it the nucleus of all sorts of folly. So it grew out of a grave! Yes, yes; and probably it would have grown out of any other dead flesh, as well as that of a human being; a dog would have answered the purpose as well as a man. You must know that the seeds of fungi are scattered so universally over the world that, only comply with the conditions, and you will produce them everywhere. Prepare the bed it loves, and a mushroom will spring up spontaneously, an excellent food, like manna from heaven. So superstition says, kill your deadliest enemy, and plant him, and he will come up in a delicious fungus, which I presume to be this; steep him, or distil him, and he will make an elixir of life for you. I suppose there is some foolish symbolism or other about the matter; but the fact I affirm to be nonsense. Dead flesh under some certain conditions of rain and sunshine, not at present ascertained by science, will produce the fungus, whether the manure be friend, or foe, or cattle."

"And as to its medical efficacy?" asked Septimius.

"That may be great for aught I know," said Portsoaken; "but I am content with my cobwebs. You may seek it out for yourself. But if the poor fellow lost his life in the supposition that he might be a useful ingredient in a recipe, you are rather an unscrupulous practitioner."

"The person whose mortal relics fill that grave," said Septimius, "was no enemy of mine (no private enemy, I mean, though he stood among the enemies of my country), nor had I anything to gain by his death. I strove to avoid aiming at his life, but he compelled me."

"Many a chance shot brings down the bird," said Doctor Portsoaken. "You say you had no interest in his death. We shall see that in the end."

Septimius did not try to follow the conversation among the mysterious hints with which the doctor chose to involve it; but he now sought to gain some information from him as to the mode of preparing the recipe, and whether he thought it would be most efficacious as a decoction, or as a distillation. The learned chemist supported most decidedly the latter opinion, and showed Septimius how he might make for himself a simpler apparatus, with no better aids than Aunt Keziah's teakettle, and one or two trifling things, which the doctor himself supplied, by which all might be done with every necessary scrupulousness.

"Let me look again at the formula," said he. "There are a good many minute directions that appear trifling, but it is not safe to neglect any minutiae in the preparation of an affair like this; because, as it is all mysterious and unknown ground together, we cannot tell which may be the important and efficacious part. For instance, when all else is done, the recipe is to be exposed seven days to the sun at noon. That does not look very important, but it may be. Then again, 'Steep it in moonlight during the second quarter.' That's all moonshine, one would think; but there's no saying. It is singular, with such preciseness, that no distinct directions are given whether to infuse, decoct, distil, or what other way; but my advice is to distil."

"I will do it," said Septimius, "and not a direction shall be neglected."

"I shall be curious to know the result," said Doctor Portsoaken, "and am glad to see the zeal with which you enter into the matter. A very valuable medicine may be recovered to science through your agency, and you may make your fortune by it; though, for my part, I prefer to trust to my cobwebs. This spider, now, is not he a lovely object? See, he is quite capable of knowledge and affection."

There seemed, in fact, to be some mode of communication between the doctor and his spider, for on some sign given by the former, imperceptible to Septimius, the many-legged monster let himself down by a cord, which he extemporized out of his own bowels, and came dangling his huge bulk down before his master's face, while the latter lavished many epithets of endearment upon him, ludicrous, and not without horror, as applied to such a hideous production of nature.

119

"I assure you," said Dr. Portsoaken, "I run some risk from my intimacy with this lovely jewel, and if I behave not all the more prudently, your countrymen will hang me for a wizard, and annihilate this precious spider as my familiar. There would be a loss to the world; not small in my own case, but enormous in the case of the spider. Look at him now, and see if the mere uninstructed observation does not discover a wonderful value in him."

In truth, when looked at closely, the spider really showed that a care and art had been bestowed upon his make, not merely as regards curiosity, but absolute beauty, that seemed to indicate that he must be a rather distinguished creature in the view of Providence; so variegated was he with a thousand minute spots, spots of color, glorious radiance, and such a brilliance was attained by many conglomerated brilliancies; and it was very strange that all this care was bestowed on a creature that, probably, had never been carefully considered except by the two pair of eyes that were now upon it; and that, in spite of its beauty and magnificence, could only be looked at with an effort to overcome the mysterious repulsiveness of its presence; for all the time that Septimius looked and admired, he still hated the thing, and thought it wrong that it was ever born, and wished that it could be annihilated. Whether the spider was conscious of the wish, we are unable to say; but certainly Septimius felt as if he were hostile to him, and had a mind to sting him; and, in fact, Dr. Portsoaken seemed of the same opinion.

"Aha, my friend," said he, "I would advise you not to come too near Orontes! He is a lovely beast, it is true; but in a certain recess of this splendid form of his he keeps a modest supply of a certain potent and piercing poison, which would produce a wonderful effect on any flesh to which he chose to apply it. A powerful fellow is Orontes; and he has a great sense of his own dignity and importance, and will not allow it to be imposed on."

Septimius moved from the vicinity of the spider, who, in fact, retreated, by climbing up his cord, and ensconced himself in the middle of his web, where he remained waiting for his prey. Septimius wondered whether the doctor were symbolized by the spider, and was likewise waiting in the middle of his web for his prey. As he saw no way, however, in which the doctor could make a profit out of himself, or how he could be victimized, the thought did not much disturb his equanimity. He was about to take his leave, but the doctor, in a derisive kind of way, bade him sit still, for he purposed keeping him as a guest, that night, at least.

"I owe you a dinner," said he, "and will pay it with a supper and knowledge; and before we part I have certain inquiries to make, of which you may not at first see the object, but yet are not quite purposeless. My familiar, up aloft there, has whispered me something about you, and I rely greatly on his intimations."

Septimius, who was sufficiently common-sensible, and invulnerable to superstitious influences on every point except that to which he had surrendered himself, was easily prevailed upon to stay; for he found the singular, charlatanic, mysterious lore of the man curious, and he had enough of real science to at least make him an object of interest to one who knew nothing of the matter; and Septimius's acuteness, too, was piqued in trying to make out what manner of man he really was, and how much in him was genuine science and self-belief, and how much quackery and pretension and conscious empiricism. So he stayed, and supped with the doctor at a table heaped more bountifully, and with rarer dainties, than Septimius had ever before conceived of; and in his simpler cognizance, heretofore, of eating merely to live, he could not but wonder to see a man of thought caring to eat of more than one dish, so that most of the meal, on his part, was spent in seeing the doctor feed and hearing him discourse upon his food.

"If man lived only to eat," quoth the doctor, "one life would not suffice, not merely to exhaust the pleasure of it, but even to get the rudiments of it."

When this important business was over, the doctor and his guest sat down again in his laboratory, where the former took care to have his usual companion, the black bottle, at his elbow, and filled his pipe, and seemed to feel a certain sullen, genial, fierce, brutal, kindly mood enough, and looked at Septimius with a sort of friendship, as if he had as lief shake hands with him as knock him down.

"Now for a talk about business," said he.

Septimius thought, however, that the doctor's talk began, at least, at a sufficient remoteness from any practical business; for he began to question about his remote ancestry, what he knew, or what record had been preserved, of the first emigrant from England; whence, from what shire or part of England, that ancestor had come; whether there were any memorial of any kind remaining of him, any letters or written documents, wills, deeds, or other legal paper; in short, all about him.

Septimius could not satisfactorily see whether these inquiries were made with any definite purpose, or from a mere general curiosity to discover how a family of early settlement in America might still be linked with the old country; whether there were any tendrils stretching across the gulf of a hundred and fifty years by which the American branch of the family was separated from the trunk of the family tree in England. The doctor partly explained this.

"You must know," said he, "that the name you bear, Felton, is one formerly of much eminence and repute in my part of England, and, indeed, very recently possessed of wealth and station. I should like to know if you are of that race."

Septimius answered with such facts and traditions as had come to his knowledge respecting his family history; a sort of history that is quite as liable to be mythical, in its early and distant stages, as that of Rome, and, indeed, seldom goes three or four generations back without getting into a mist really impenetrable, though great, gloomy, and magnificent shapes of men often seem to loom in it, who, if they could be brought close to the naked eye, would turn out as commonplace as the descendants who wonder at and admire them. He remembered Aunt Keziah's legend and said he had reason to believe that his first ancestor came over at a somewhat earlier date than the first Puritan settlers, and dwelt among the Indians where (and here the young man cast down his eyes, having the customary American abhorrence for any mixture of blood) he had intermarried with the daughter of a sagamore, and succeeded to his rule. This might have happened as early as the end of Elizabeth's reign, perhaps later. It was impossible to decide dates on such a matter. There had been a son of this connection, perhaps more than one, but certainly one son, who, on the arrival of the Puritans, was a youth, his father appearing to have been slain in some outbreak of the tribe, perhaps owing to the jealousy of prominent chiefs at seeing their natural authority abrogated or absorbed by a man of different race. He slightly alluded to the supernatural attributes that gathered round this predecessor, but in a way to imply that he put no faith in them; for Septimius's natural keen sense and perception kept him from betraying his weaknesses to the doctor, by the same instinctive and subtle caution with which a madman can so well conceal his infirmity.

On the arrival of the Puritans, they had found among the Indians a youth partly of their own blood, able, though imperfectly, to speak their language,—having, at least, some early recollections of it,—inheriting, also, a share of influence over the tribe on which his father had grafted him. It was natural that they should pay especial attention to this youth, consider it their duty to give him religious instruction in the faith of his fathers, and try to use him as a means of influencing his tribe. They did so, but did not succeed in swaying the tribe by his means, their success having been limited to winning the half-Indian from the wild ways of his mother's people, into a certain partial, but decent accommodation to those of the English. A tendency to civilization was brought out in his character by their rigid training; at least, his savage wildness was broken. He built a house among them, with a good deal of the wigwam, no doubt, in its style of architecture, but still a permanent house, near which he established a corn-field, a pumpkin-garden, a melon-patch, and became farmer enough to be entitled to ask the hand of a Puritan maiden. There he spent his life, with some few instances of temporary relapse into savage wildness, when he fished in the river Musquehannah, or in Walden, or strayed in the woods, when he should have been planting or hoeing; but, on the whole, the race had been redeemed from barbarism in his person, and in the succeeding generations had been tamed more and more. The second generation had been distinguished in the Indian wars of the provinces, and then intermarried with the stock of a distinguished Puritan divine, by which means Septimius could reckon great and learned men, scholars of old Cambridge, among his ancestry on one side, while on the other it ran up to the early emigrants, who seemed to have been remarkable men, and to that strange wild lineage of Indian chiefs, whose blood was like that of persons not quite human, intermixed with civilized blood.

"I wonder," said the doctor, musingly, "whether there are really no documents to ascertain the epoch at which that old first emigrant came over, and whence he came, and precisely from what English family. Often the last heir of some respectable name dies in England, and we say that the family is extinct; whereas, very possibly, it may be abundantly flourishing in the New World, revived by the rich infusion of new blood in a new soil, instead of growing feebler, heavier, stupider, each year by sticking to an old soil, intermarrying over and over again with the same respectable families, till it has made common stock of all their vices, weaknesses, madnesses. Have you no documents, I say, no muniment deed?"

"None," said Septimius.

"No old furniture, desks, trunks, chests, cabinets?"

"You must remember," said Septimius, "that my Indian ancestor was not very likely to have brought such things out of the forest with him. A wandering Indian does not carry a chest of papers with him. I do remember, in my childhood, a little old iron-bound chest, or coffer, of which the key was lost, and which my Aunt Keziah used to say came down from her great-great-grandfather. I don't know what has become of it, and my poor old aunt kept it among her own treasures."

"Well, my friend, do you hunt up that old coffer, and, just as a matter of curiosity, let me see the contents."

"I have other things to do," said Septimius.

"Perhaps so," quoth the doctor, "but no other, as it may turn out, of quite so much importance as this. I'll tell you fairly: the heir of a great English house is lately dead, and the estate lies open to any well-sustained, perhaps to any plausible, claimant. If it should appear from the records of that family, as I have some reason to suppose, that a member of it, who would now represent the older branch, disappeared mysteriously and unaccountably, at a date corresponding with what might be ascertained as that of your ancestor's first appearance in this country; if any reasonable proof can be brought forward, on the part of the representatives of that white sagamore, that wizard powwow, or however you call him, that he was the disappearing Englishman, why, a good case is made out. Do you feel no interest in such a prospect?"

"Very little, I confess," said Septimius.

"Very little!" said the grim doctor, impatiently. "Do not you see that, if you make good your claim, you establish for yourself a position among the English aristocracy, and succeed to a noble English estate, an ancient hall, where your forefathers have dwelt since the Conqueror; splendid gardens, hereditary woods and parks, to which anything America can show is despicable,—all thoroughly cultivated and adorned, with the care and ingenuity of centuries; and an income, a month of which would be greater wealth than any of your American ancestors, raking and scraping for his lifetime, has ever got together, as the accumulated result of the toil and penury by which he has sacrificed body and soul?"

"That strain of Indian blood is in me yet," said Septimius, "and it makes me despise,—no, not despise; for I can see their desirableness for other people,—but it makes me reject for myself what you think so valuable. I do not care for these common aims. I have ambition, but it is for prizes such as other men cannot gain, and do not think of aspiring after. I could not live in the habits of English life, as I conceive it to be, and would not, for my part, be burdened with the great estate you speak of. It might answer my purpose for a time. It would suit me well enough to try that mode of life, as well as a hundred others, but only for a time. It is of no permanent importance."

"I'll tell you what it is, young man," said the doctor, testily, "you have something in your brain that makes you talk very foolishly; and I have partly a suspicion what it is,—only I can't think that a fellow who is really gifted with respectable sense, in other directions, should be such a confounded idiot in this."

Septimius blushed, but held his peace, and the conversation languished after this; the doctor grimly smoking his pipe, and by no means increasing the milkiness of his mood by frequent applications to the black bottle, until Septimius intimated that he would like to go to bed. The old woman was summoned, and ushered him to his chamber.

At breakfast, the doctor partially renewed the subject which he seemed to consider most important in yesterday's conversation.

"My young friend," said he, "I advise you to look in cellar and garret, or wherever you consider the most likely place, for that iron-bound coffer. There may be nothing in it; it may be full of musty love-letters, or old sermons, or receipted bills of a hundred years ago; but it may contain what will be worth to you an estate of five thousand pounds a year. It is a pity the old woman with the damnable decoction is gone off. Look it up, I say."

"Well, well," said Septimius, abstractedly, "when I can find time."

So saying, he took his leave, and retraced his way back to his home. He had not seemed like himself during the time that elapsed since he left it, and it appeared an infinite space that he had lived through and travelled over, and he fancied it hardly possible that he could ever get back again. But now, with every step that he took, he found himself getting miserably back into the old enchanted land. The mist rose up about him, the pale mist-bow of ghostly promise curved before him; and he trod back again, poor boy, out of the clime of real effort, into the land of his dreams and shadowy enterprise.

"How was it," said he, "that I can have been so untrue to my convictions? Whence came that dark and dull despair that weighed upon me? Why did I let the mocking mood which I was conscious of in that brutal, brandy-burnt sceptic have such an influence on me? Let him guzzle! He shall not tempt me from my pursuit, with his lure of an estate and name among those heavy English beef-eaters of whom he is a brother. My destiny is one which kings might envy, and strive in vain to buy with principalities and kingdoms."

So he trod on air almost, in the latter parts of his journey, and instead of being wearied, grew more airy with the latter miles that brought him to his wayside home.

So now Septimius sat down and began in earnest his endeavors and experiments to prepare the medicine, according to the mysterious terms of the recipe. It seemed not possible to do it, so many rebuffs and disappointments did he meet with. No effort would produce a combination answering to the

126

description of the recipe, which propounded a brilliant, gold-colored liquid, clear as the air itself, with a certain fragrance which was peculiar to it, and also, what was the more individual test of the correctness of the mixture, a certain coldness of the feeling, a chillness which was described as peculiarly refreshing and invigorating. With all his trials, he produced nothing but turbid results, clouded generally, or lacking something in color, and never that fragrance, and never that coldness which was to be the test of truth. He studied all the books of chemistry which at that period were attainable,–a period when, in the world, it was a science far unlike what it has since become; and when Septimius had no instruction in this country, nor could obtain any beyond the dark, mysterious charlatanic communications of Doctor Portsoaken. So that, in fact, he seemed to be discovering for himself the science through which he was to work. He seemed to do everything that was stated in the recipe, and yet no results came from it; the liquid that he produced was nauseous to the smell,–to taste it he had a horrible repugnance, turbid, nasty, reminding him in most respects of poor Aunt Keziah's elixir; and it was a body without a soul, and that body dead. And so it went on; and the poor, half-maddened Septimius began to think that his immortal life was preserved by the mere effort of seeking for it, but was to be spent in the quest, and was therefore to be made an eternity of abortive misery. He pored over the document that had so possessed him, turning its crabbed meanings every way, trying to get out of it some new light, often tempted to fling it into the fire which he kept under his retort, and let the whole thing go; but then again, soon rising out of that black depth of despair, into a determination to do what he had so long striven for. With such intense action of mind as he brought to bear on this paper, it is wonderful that it was not spiritually distilled; that its essence did not arise, purified from all alloy of falsehood, from all turbidness of obscurity and ambiguity, and form a pure essence of truth and invigorating motive, if of any it were capable. In this interval, Septimius is said by tradition to have found out many wonderful secrets that were almost beyond the scope of science. It was said that old Aunt Keziah used to come with a coal of fire from unknown furnaces, to light his distilling apparatus; it was said, too, that the ghost of the old lord, whose ingenuity had propounded this puzzle for his descendants, used to come at midnight and strive to explain to him this manuscript; that the Black Man, too, met him on the hill-top, and promised him an immediate release from his difficulties, provided he would kneel down and worship him, and sign his name in his book, an old, iron-clasped, much-worn volume, which he produced from his ample pockets, and showed him in it the names of many a man whose name has become historic, and above whose ashes kept watch an inscription testifying to his virtues and devotion,–old autographs,–for the Black Man was the original autograph collector.

But these, no doubt, were foolish stories, conceived and propagated in chimney-corners, while yet there were chimney-corners and firesides, and smoky flues. There was no truth in such things, I am sure; the Black Man had changed his tactics, and knew better than to lure the human soul thus to come to him with his musty autograph-book. So Septimiusfought with his difficulty by himself, as many a beginner inscience has done before him; and to his efforts in this way are popularly attributed many herb-drinks, and some kinds of spruce-beer, and nostrums used for rheumatism, sore throat,and typhus fever; but I rather think they all came from Aunt Keziah; or perhaps, like jokes to Joe Miller, all sorts of quack medicines, flocking at large through the community, are assigned to him or her. The people have a little mistaken the character and purpose of poor Septimius, and remember him as a quack doctor, instead of a seeker for a secret, not the less sublime and elevating because it happened to be unattainable.

I know not through what medium or by what means, but it got noised abroad that Septimius was engaged in some mysterious work; and, indeed, his seclusion, his absorption, his indifference to all that was going on in that weary time of war, looked strange enough to indicate that it must be some most important business that engrossed him. On the few occasions when he came out from his immediate haunts into the village, he had a strange, owl-like appearance, uncombed, unbrushed, his hair long and tangled; his face, they said, darkened with smoke; his cheeks pale; the indentation of his brow deeper than ever before; an earnest, haggard, sulking look; and so he went hastily along the village street, feeling as if all eyes might find out what he had in his mind from his appearance; taking by-ways where they were to be found, going long distances through woods and fields, rather than short ones

128

where the way lay through the frequented haunts of men. For he shunned the glances of his fellow-men, probably because he had learnt to consider them not as fellows, because he was seeking to withdraw himself from the common bond and destiny,–because he felt, too, that on that account his fellow-men would consider him as a traitor, an enemy, one who had deserted their cause, and tried to withdraw his feeble shoulder from under that great burden of death which is imposed on all men to bear, and which, if one could escape, each other would feel his load propertionably heavier. With these beings of a moment he had no longer any common cause; they must go their separate ways, yet apparently the same,–they on the broad, dusty, beaten path, that seemed always full, but from which continually they so strangely vanished into invisibility, no one knowing, nor long inquiring, what had become of them; he on his lonely path, where he should tread secure, with no trouble but the loneliness, which would be none to him. For a little while he would seem to keep them company, but soon they would all drop away, the minister, his accustomed towns-people, Robert Hagburn, Rose, Sibyl Dacy,–all leaving him in blessed unknownness to adopt new temporary relations, and take a new course.

Sometimes, however, the prospect a little chilled him. Could he give them all up,–the sweet sister; the friend of his childhood; the grave instructor of his youth; the homely, life-known faces? Yes; there were such rich possibilities in the future: for he would seek out the noblest minds, the deepest hearts in every age, and be the friend of human time. Only it might be sweet to have one unchangeable companion; for, unless he strung the pearls and diamonds of life upon one unbroken affection, he sometimes thought that his life would have nothing to give it unity and identity; and so the longest life would be but an aggregate of insulated fragments, which would have no relation to one another. And so it would not be one life, but many unconnected ones. Unless he could look into the same eyes, through the mornings of future time, opening and blessing him with the fresh gleam of love and joy; unless the same sweet voice could melt his thoughts together; unless some sympathy of a life side by side with his could knit them into one; looking back upon the same things, looking forward to the same; the long, thin thread of an individual life, stretching onward and onward, would cease to be visible, cease to be felt, cease, by and by, to have any real bigness in proportion to its length, and so be virtually non-existent, except in the mere inconsiderable Now. If a group of chosen friends, chosen out of all the world for their adaptedness, could go on in endless life together, keeping themselves mutually warm on the high, desolate way, then none of them need ever sigh to be comforted in the pitiable snugness of the grave. If one especial soul might be his companion, then how complete the fence of mutual arms, the warmth of close-pressing breast to breast! Might there be one! O Sibyl Dacy!

Perhaps it could not be. Who but himself could undergo that great trial, and hardship, and self-denial, and firm purpose, never wavering, never sinking for a moment, keeping his grasp on life like one who holds up by main force a sinking and drowning friend?–how could a woman do it! He must then give up the thought. There was a choice,–friendship, and the love of woman,–the long life of immortality. There was something heroic and ennobling in choosing the latter. And so he walked with the mysterious girl on the hill-top, and sat down beside her on the grave, which still ceased not to redden, portentously beautiful, with that unnatural flower,–and they talked together; and Septimius looked on her weird beauty, and often said to himself, "This, too, will pass away; she is not capable of what I am; she is a woman. It must be a manly and courageous and forcible spirit, vastly rich in all three particulars, that has strength enough to live! Ah, is it surely so? There is such a dark sympathy between us, she knows me so well, she touches my inmost so at unawares, that I could almost think I had a companion here. Perhaps not so soon. At the end of centuries I might wed one; not now."

But once he said to Sibyl Dacy, "Ah, how sweet it would be–sweet for me, at least–if this intercourse might last forever!"

"That is an awful idea that you present," said Sibyl, with a hardly perceptible, involuntary shudder; "always on this hill-top, always passing and repassing this little hillock; always smelling these flowers! I always looking at this deep chasm in your brow; you always seeing my bloodless cheek!–doing this till these trees crumble away, till perhaps a new forest grew up wherever this white race had planted, and a race of savages again possess the soil. I should not like it. My mission here is but for a short time, and will soon be accomplished, and then I go."

"You do not rightly estimate the way in which the long time might be spent," said Septimius. "We would find out a thousand uses of this world, uses and enjoyments which now men never dream of, because the world is just held to their mouths, and then snatched away again, before they have time hardly to taste it, instead of becoming acquainted with the deliciousness of this great world-fruit. But you speak of a mission, and as if you were now in performance of it. Will you not tell me what it is?"

"No," said Sibyl Dacy, smiling on him. "But one day you shall know what it is,–none sooner nor better than you,–so much I promise you."

"Are we friends?" asked Septimius, somewhat puzzled by her look.

"We have an intimate relation to one another," replied Sibyl.

"And what is it?" demanded Septimius.

"That will appear hereafter," answered Sibyl, again smiling on him.

He knew not what to make of this, nor whether to be exalted or depressed; but, at all events, there seemed to be an accordance, a striking together, a mutual touch of their two natures, as if, somehow or other, they were performing the same part of solemn music; so that he felt his soul thrill, and at the same time shudder. Some sort of sympathy there surely was, but of what nature he could not tell; though often he was impelled to ask himself the same question he asked Sibyl, "Are we friends?" because of a sudden shock and repulsion that came between them, and passed away in a moment; and there would be Sibyl, smiling askance on him.

And then he toiled away again at his chemical pursuits; tried to mingle things harmoniously that apparently were not born to be mingled; discovering a science for himself, and mixing it up with absurdities that other chemists had long ago flung aside; but still there would be that turbid aspect, still that lack of fragrance, still that want of the peculiar temperature, that was announced as the test of the matter. Over and over again he set the crystal vase in the sun, and let it stay there the appointed time, hoping that it would digest in such a manner as to bring about the desired result.

One day, as it happened, his eyes fell upon the silver key which he had taken from the breast of the dead young man, and he thought within himself that this might have something to do with the seemingly unattainable success of his pursuit. He remembered, for the first time, the grim doctor's emphatic injunction to search for the little iron-bound box of which he had spoken, and which had come down with such legends attached to it; as, for instance, that it held the Devil's bond with his great-great-grandfather, now cancelled by the surrender of the latter's soul; that it held the golden key of Paradise; that it was full of old gold, or of the dry leaves of a hundred years ago; that it had a familiar fiend in it, who would be exorcised by the turning of the lock, but would otherwise remain a prisoner till the solid oak of the box mouldered, or the iron rusted away; so that between fear and the loss of the key, this curious old box had remained unopened, till itself was lost.

But now Septimius, putting together what Aunt Keziah had said in her dying moments, and what Doctor Portsoaken had insisted upon, suddenly came to the conclusion that the possession of the old iron box might be of the greatest importance to him. So he set himself at once to think where he had last seen it. Aunt Keziah, of course, had put it away in some safe place or other, either in cellar or garret, no doubt; so Septimius, in the intervals of his other occupations, devoted several days to the search; and not to weary the reader with the particulars of the quest for an old box, suffice it to say that he at last found it, amongst various other antique rubbish, in a corner of the garret.

It was a very rusty old thing, not more than a foot in length, and half as much in height and breadth; but most ponderously iron-bound, with bars, and corners, and all sorts of fortification; looking very much like an ancient alms-box, such as are to be seen in the older rural churches of England, and which seem to intimate great distrust of those to whom the funds are committed. Indeed, there might be a shrewd suspicion that some ancient church beadle among Septimius's forefathers, when emigrating from England, had taken the opportunity of bringing the poor-box along with him. On looking close, too, there were rude embellishments on the lid and sides of the box in long-rusted steel, designs such as the Middle Ages were rich in; a representation of Adam and Eve, or of Satan and a soul, nobody could tell which; but, at any rate, an illustration of great value and interest. Septimius looked at this ugly, rusty, ponderous old box, so worn and battered with time, and recollected with a scornful smile the legends of which it was the object; all of which he despised and discredited, just as much as he did that story in the "Arabian Nights," where a demon comes out of a copper vase, in a cloud of smoke that covers the sea-shore; for he was singularly invulnerable to all modes of superstition, all nonsense, except his own. But that one mode was ever in full force and operation with him. He felt strongly convinced that inside the old box was something that appertained to his destiny; the key that he had taken from the dead man's breast, had that come down through time, and across the sea, and had a man died to bring and deliver it to him, merely for nothing? It could not be.

He looked at the old, rusty, elaborated lock of the little receptacle. It was much flourished about with what was once polished steel; and certainly, when thus polished, and the steel bright with which it was hooped, defended, and inlaid, it must have been a thing fit to appear in any cabinet; though now the oak was worm-eaten as an old coffin, and the rust of the iron came off red on Septimius's fingers, after he had been fumbling at it. He looked at the curious old silver key, too, and fancied that he discovered in its elaborate handle some likeness to the ornaments about the box; at any rate, this he determined was the key of fate, and he was just applying it to the lock when somebody tapped familiarly at the door, having opened the outer one, and stepped in with a manly stride. Septimius, inwardly blaspheming, as secluded men are apt to do when any interruption comes, and especially when it comes at some critical moment of projection, left the box as yet unbroached, and said, "Come in."

The door opened, and Robert Hagburn entered; looking so tall and stately, that Septimius hardly knew him for the youth with whom he had grown up familiarly. He had on the Revolutionary dress of buff and blue, with decorations that to the initiated eye denoted him an officer, and certainly there was a kind of authority in his look and manner, indicating that heavy responsibilities, critical moments, had educated him, and turned the ploughboy into a man.

"Is it you?" exclaimed Septimius. "I scarcely knew you. How war has altered you!"

"And I may say, Is it you? for you are much altered likewise, my old friend. Study wears upon you terribly. You will be an old man, at this rate, before you know you are a young one. You will kill yourself, as sure as a gun!"

"Do you think so?" said Septimius, rather startled, for the queer absurdity of the position struck him, if he should so exhaust and wear himself as to die, just at the moment when he should have found out the secret of everlasting life. "But though I look pale, I am very vigorous. Judging from that scar, slanting down from your temple, you have been nearer death than you now think me, though in another way."

"Yes," said Robert Hagburn; "but in hot blood, and for a good cause, who cares for death? And yet I love life; none better, while it lasts, and I love it in all its looks and turns and surprises,–there is so much to be got out of it, in spite of all that people say. Youth is sweet, with its fiery enterprise, and I suppose mature manhood will be just as much so, though in a calmer way, and age, quieter still, will have its own merits,–the thing is only to do with life what we ought, and what is suited to each of its stages; do all, enjoy all,–and I suppose these two rules amount to the same thing. Only catch real earnest hold of life, not play with it, and not defer one part of it for the sake of another, then each part of life will do for us what was intended. People talk of the hardships of military service, of the miseries that we undergo fighting for our country. I have undergone my share, I believe,–hard toil in the wilderness, hunger, extreme weariness, pinching cold, the torture of a wound, peril of death; and really I have been as happy through it as ever I was at my mother's cosey fireside of a winter's evening. If I had died, I doubt not my last moments would have been happy. There is no use of life, but just to find out what is fit for us to do; and, doing it, it seems to be little matter whether we live or die in it. God does not want our work, but only our willingness to work; at least, the last seems to answer all his purposes."

"This is a comfortable philosophy of yours," said Septimius, rather contemptuously, and yet enviously. "Where did you get it, Robert?"

"Where? Nowhere; it came to me on the march; and though I can't say that I thought it when the bullets pattered into the snow about me, in those narrow streets of Quebec, yet, I suppose, it was in my mind then; for, as I tell you, I was very cheerful and contented. And you, Septimius? I never saw such a discontented, unhappy-looking fellow as you are. You have had a harder time in peace than I in war. You have not found what you seek, whatever that may be. Take my advice. Give yourself to the next work that comes to hand. The war offers place to all of us; we ought to be thankful,–the most joyous of all the generations before or after us,–since Providence gives us such good work to live for, or such a good opportunity to die. It is worth living for, just to have the chance to die so well as a man may in these days. Come, be a soldier. Be a chaplain, since your education lies that way; and you will find that nobody in peace prays so well as we do, we soldiers; and you shall not be debarred from fighting, too; if war is holy work, a priest may lawfully do it, as well as pray for it. Come with us, my old friend Septimius, be my comrade, and, whether you live or die, you will thank me for getting you out of the yellow forlornness in which you go on, neither living nor dying."

Septimius looked at Robert Hagburn in surprise; so much was he altered and improved by this brief experience of war, adventure, responsibility, which he had passed through. Not less than the effect produced on his loutish, rustic air and deportment, developing his figure, seeming to make him taller, setting free the manly graces that lurked within his awkward frame,–not less was the effect on his mind and moral nature, giving freedom of ideas, simple perception of great thoughts, a free natural chivalry; so that the knight, the Homeric warrior, the hero, seemed to be here, or possible to be here, in the young New England rustic; and all that history has given, and hearts throbbed and sighed and gloried over, of patriotism and heroic feeling and action, might be repeated, perhaps, in the life and death of this familiar friend and playmate of his, whom he had valued not over highly,–Robert Hagburn. He had merely followed out his natural heart, boldly and singly,–doing the first good thing that came to hand,–and here was a hero.

"You almost make me envy you, Robert," said he, sighing.

"Then why not come with me?" asked Robert.

"Because I have another destiny," said Septimius.

"Well, you are mistaken; be sure of that," said Robert. "This is not a generation for study, and the making of books; that may come by and by. This great fight has need of all men to carry it on, in one way or another; and no man will do well, even for himself, who tries to avoid his share in it. But I have said my say. And now, Septimius, the war takes much of a man, but it does not take him all, and what it leaves is all the more full of life and health thereby. I have something to say to you about this."

"Say it then, Robert," said Septimius, who, having got over the first excitement of the interview, and the sort of exhilaration produced by the healthful glow of Robert's spirit, began secretly to wish that it might close, and to be permitted to return to his solitary thoughts again. "What can I do for you?"

"Why, nothing," said Robert, looking rather confused, "since all is settled. The fact is, my old friend, as perhaps you have seen, I have very long had an eye upon your sister Rose; yes, from the time we went together to the old school-house, where she now teaches children like what we were then. The war took me away, and in good time, for I doubt if Rose would ever have cared enough for me to be my wife, if I had stayed at home, a country lout, as I was getting to be, in shirt-sleeves and bare feet. But now, you see, I have come back, and this whole great war, to her woman's heart, is represented in me, and makes me heroic, so to speak, and strange, and yet her old familiar lover. So I found her heart tenderer for me than it was; and, in short, Rose has consented to be my wife, and we mean to be married in a week; my furlough permits little delay."

"You surprise me," said Septimius, who, immersed in his own pursuits, had taken no notice of the growing affection between Robert and his sister. "Do you think it well to snatch this little lull that is allowed you in the wild striving of war to try to make a peaceful home? Shall you like to be summoned from it soon? Shall you be as cheerful among dangers afterwards, when one sword may cut down two happinesses?"

"There is something in what you say, and I have thought of it," said Robert, sighing. "But I can't tell how it is; but there is something in this uncertainty, this peril, this cloud before us, that makes it sweeter to love and to be loved than amid all seeming quiet and serenity. Really, I think, if there were to be no death, the beauty of life would be all tame. So we take our chance, or our dispensation of Providence, and are going to love, and to be married, just as confidently as if we were sure of living forever."

"Well, old fellow," said Septimius, with more cordiality and outgush of heart than he had felt for a long while, "there is no man whom I should be happier to call brother. Take Rose, and all happiness along with her. She is a good girl, and not in the least like me. May you live out your threescore years and ten, and every one of them be happy."

Little more passed, and Robert Hagburn took his leave with a hearty shake of Septimius's hand, too conscious of his own happiness to be quite sensible how much the latter was self-involved, strange, anxious, separated from healthy life and interests; and Septimius, as soon as Robert had disappeared, locked the door behind him, and proceeded at once to apply the silver key to the lock of the old strong box.

The lock resisted somewhat, being rusty, as might well be supposed after so many years since it was opened; but it finally allowed the key to turn, and Septimius, with a good deal of flutter at his heart, opened the lid. The interior had a very different aspect from that of the exterior; for, whereas the latter looked so old, this, having been kept from the air, looked about as new as when shut up from light and air two centuries ago, less or more. It was lined with ivory, beautifully carved in figures, according to the art which the mediæval people possessed in great perfection; and probably the box had been a lady's jewel-casket formerly, and had glowed with rich lustre and bright colors at former openings. But now there was nothing in it of that kind,– nothing in keeping with those figures carved in the ivory representing some mythical subjects,–nothing but some papers in the bottom of the box written over in an ancient hand, which Septimius at once fancied that he recognized as that of the manuscript and recipe which he had found on the breast of the young soldier. He eagerly seized them, but was infinitely disappointed to find that they did not seem to refer at all to the subjects treated by the former, but related to pedigrees and genealogies, and were in reference to an English family and some member of it who, two centuries before, had crossed the sea to America, and who, in this way, had sought to preserve his connection with his native stock, so as to be able, perhaps, to prove it for himself or his descendants; and there was reference to documents and records in England in confirmation of the genealogy. Septimius saw that this paper had been drawn up by an ancestor of his own, the unfortunate man who had been hanged for witchcraft; but so earnest had been his expectation of something different, that he flung the old papers down with bitter indifference.

Then again he snatched them up, and contemptuously read them,— those proofs of descent through generations of esquires and knights, who had been renowned in war; and there seemed, too, to be running through the family a certain tendency to letters, for three were designated as of the colleges of Oxford or Cambridge; and against one there was the note, "he that sold himself to Sathan;" and another seemed to have been a follower of Wickliffe; and they had murdered kings, and been beheaded, and banished, and what not; so that the age-long life of this ancient family had not been after all a happy or very prosperous one, though they had kept their estate, in one or another descendant, since the Conquest. It was not wholly without interest that Septimius saw that this ancient descent, this connection with noble families, and intermarriages with names, some of which he recognized as known in English history, all referred to his own family, and seemed to centre in himself, the last of a poverty-stricken line, which had dwindled down into obscurity, and into rustic labor and humble toil, reviving in him a little; yet how little, unless he fulfilled his strange purpose. Was it not better worth his while to take this English position here so strangely offered him? He had apparently slain unwittingly the only person who could have contested his rights,—the young man who had so strangely brought him the hope of unlimited life at the same time that he was making room for him among his forefathers. What a change in his lot would have been here, for there seemed to be some pretensions to a title, too, from a barony which was floating about and occasionally moving out of abeyancy!

"Perhaps," said Septimius to himself, "I may hereafter think it worth while to assert my claim to these possessions, to this position amid an ancient aristocracy, and try that mode of life for one generation. Yet there is something in my destiny incompatible, of course, with the continued possession of an estate. I must be, of necessity, a wanderer on the face of the earth, changing place at short intervals, disappearing suddenly and entirely; else the foolish, short-lived multitude and mob of mortals will be enraged with one who seems their brother, yet whose countenance will never be furrowed with his age, nor his knees totter, nor his force be abated; their little brevity will be rebuked by his age-long endurance, above whom the oaken roof-tree of a thousand years would crumble, while still he would be hale and strong. So that this house, or any other, would be but a resting-place of a day, and then I must away into another obscurity."

With almost a regret, he continued to look over the documents until he reached one of the persons recorded in the line of pedigree,–a worthy, apparently, of the reign of Elizabeth, to whom was attributed a title of Doctor in Utriusque Juris; and against his name was a verse of Latin written, for what purpose Septimius knew not, for, on reading it, it appeared to have no discoverable appropriateness; but suddenly he remembered the blotted and imperfect hieroglyphical passage in the recipe. He thought an instant, and was convinced this was the full expression and outwriting of that crabbed little mystery; and that here was part of that secret writing for which the Age of Elizabeth was so famous and so dexterous. His mind had a flash of light upon it, and from that moment he was enabled to read not only the recipe but the rules, and all the rest of that mysterious document, in a way which he had never thought of before; to discern that it was not to be taken literally and simply, but had a hidden process involved in it that made the whole thing infinitely deeper than he had hitherto deemed it to be. His brain reeled, he seemed to have taken a draught of some liquor that opened infinite depths before him, he could scarcely refrain from giving a shout of triumphant exultation, the house could not contain him, he rushed up to his hill-top, and there, after walking swiftly to and fro, at length flung himself on the little hillock, and burst forth, as if addressing him who slept beneath.

"O brother, O friend!" said he, "I thank thee for thy matchless beneficence to me; for all which I rewarded thee with this little spot on my hill-top. Thou wast very good, very kind. It would not have been well for thee, a youth of fiery joys and passions, loving to laugh, loving the lightness and sparkling brilliancy of life, to take this boon to thyself; for, O brother! I see, I see, it requires a strong spirit, capable of much lonely endurance, able to be sufficient to itself, loving not too much, dependent on no sweet ties of affection, to be capable of the mighty trial which now devolves on me. I thank thee, O kinsman! Yet thou, I feel, hast the better part, who didst so soon lie down to rest, who hast done forever with this troublesome world, which it is mine to contemplate from age to age, and to sum up the meaning of it. Thou art disporting thyself in other spheres. I enjoy the high, severe, fearful office of living here, and of being the minister of Providence from one age to many successive ones."

In this manner he raved, as never before, in a strain of exalted enthusiasm, securely treading on air, and sometimes stopping to shout aloud, and feeling as if he should burst if he did not do so; and his voice came back to him again from the low hills on the other side of the broad, level valley, and out of the woods afar, mocking him; or as if it were airy spirits, that knew how it was all to be, confirming his cry, saying "It shall be so," "Thou hast found it at last," "Thou art immortal." And it seemed as if Nature were inclined to celebrate his triumph over herself; for above the woods that crowned the hill to the northward, there were shoots and streams of radiance, a white, a red, a many-colored lustre, blazing up high towards the zenith, dancing up, flitting down, dancing up again; so that it seemed as if spirits were keeping a revel there. The leaves of the trees on the hill-side, all except the evergreens, had now mostly fallen with the autumn; so that Septimius was seen by the few passers-by, in the decline of the afternoon, passing to and fro along his path, wildly gesticulating; and heard to shout so that the echoes came from all directions to answer him. After nightfall, too, in the harvest moonlight, a shadow was still seen passing there, waving its arms in shadowy triumph; so, the next day, there were various goodly stories afloat and astir, coming out of successive mouths, more wondrous at each birth; the simplest form of the story being, that Septimius Felton had at last gone raving mad on the hill-top that he was so fond of haunting; and those who listened to his shrieks said that he was calling to the Devil; and some said that by certain exorcisms he had caused the appearance of a battle in the air, charging squadrons, cannon-flashes, champions encountering; all of which foreboded some real battle to be fought with the enemies of the country; and as the battle of Monmouth chanced to occur, either the very next day, or about that time, this was supposed to be either caused or foretold by Septimius's eccentricities; and as the battle was not very favorable to our arms, the patriotism of Septimius suffered much in popular estimation.

But he knew nothing, thought nothing, cared nothing about his country, or his country's battles; he was as sane as he had been for a year past, and was wise enough, though merely by instinct, to throw off some of his superfluous excitement by these wild gestures, with wild shouts, and restless activity; and when he had partly accomplished this he returned to the house, and, late as it was, kindled his fire, and began anew the processes of chemistry, now enlightened by the late teachings. A new agent seemed to him to mix itself up with his toil and to forward his purpose; something helped him along; everything became facile to his manipulation, clear to his thought. In this way he spent the night, and when at sunrise he let in the eastern light upon his study, the thing was done.

Septimius had achieved it. That is to say, he had succeeded in amalgamating his materials so that they acted upon one another, and in accordance; and had produced a result that had a subsistence in itself, and a right to be; a something potent and substantial; each ingredient contributing its part to form a new essence, which was as real and individual as anything it was formed from. But in order to perfect it, there was necessity that the powers of nature should act quietly upon it through a month of sunshine; that the moon, too, should have its part in the production; and so he must wait patiently for this. Wait! surely he would! Had he not time for waiting? Were he to wait till old age, it would not be too much; for all future time would have it in charge to repay him.

So he poured the inestimable liquor into a glass vase, well secured from the air, and placed it in the sunshine, shifting it from one sunny window to another, in order that it might ripen; moving it gently lest he should disturb the living spirit that he knew to be in it. And he watched it from day to day, watched the reflections in it, watched its lustre, which seemed to him to grow greater day by day, as if it imbibed the sunlight into it. Never was there anything so bright as this. It changed its hue, too, gradually, being now a rich purple, now a crimson, now a violet, now a blue; going through all these prismatic colors without losing any of its brilliance, and never was there such a hue as the sunlight took in falling through it and resting on his floor. And strange and beautiful it was, too, to look through this medium at the outer world, and see how it was glorified and made anew, and did not look like the same world, although there were all its familiar marks. And then, past his window, seen through this, went the farmer and his wife, on saddle and pillion, jogging to meeting-house or market; and the very dog, the cow coming home from pasture, the old familiar faces of his childhood, looked differently. And so at last, at the end of the month, it settled into a most deep and brilliant crimson, as if it were the essence of the blood of the young man whom he had slain; the flower being now triumphant, it had given its own hue to the whole mass, and had grown brighter every day; so that it seemed to have inherent light, as if it were a planet by itself, a heart of crimson fire burning within it.

And when this had been done, and there was no more change, showing that the digestion was perfect, then he took it and placed it where the changing moon would fall upon it; and then again he watched it, covering it in darkness by day, revealing it to the moon by night; and watching it here, too, through more changes. And by and by he perceived that the deep crimson hue was departing,–not fading; we cannot say that, because of the prodigious lustre which still pervaded it, and was not less strong than ever; but certainly the hue became fainter, now a rose-color, now fainter, fainter still, till there was only left the purest whiteness of the moon itself; a change that somewhat disappointed and grieved Septimius, though still it seemed fit that the water of life should be of no one richness, because it must combine all. As the absorbed young man gazed through the lonely nights at his beloved liquor, he fancied sometimes that he could see wonderful things in the crystal sphere of the vase; as in Doctor Dee's magic crystal used to be seen, which now lies in the British Museum; representations, it might be, of things in the far past, or in the further future, scenes in which he himself was to act, persons yet unborn, the beautiful and the wise, with whom he was to be associated, palaces and towers, modes of hitherto unseen architecture, that old hall in England to which he had a hereditary right, with its gables, and its smooth lawn; the witch-meetings in which his ancestor used to take part; Aunt Keziah on her death-bed; and, flitting through all, the shade of Sibyl Dacy, eying him from secret nooks, or some remoteness, with her peculiar mischievous smile, beckoning him into the sphere. All such visions would he see, and then become aware that he had been in a dream, superinduced by too much watching, too intent thought; so that living among so many dreams, he was almost afraid that he should find himself waking out of yet another, and find that the vase itself and the liquid it contained were also dream-stuff. But no; these were real.

There was one change that surprised him, although he accepted it without doubt, and, indeed, it did imply a wonderful efficacy, at least singularity, in the newly converted liquid. It grew strangely cool in temperature in the latter part of his watching it. It appeared to imbibe its coldness from the cold, chaste moon, until it seemed to Septimius that it was colder than ice itself; the mist gathered upon the crystal vase as upon a tumbler of iced water in a warm room. Some say it actually gathered thick with frost, crystallized into a thousand fantastic and beautiful shapes, but this I do not know so well. Only it was very cold. Septimius pondered upon it, and thought he saw that life itself was cold, individual in its being, a high, pure essence, chastened from all heats; cold, therefore, and therefore invigorating.

Thus much, inquiring deeply, and with painful research into the liquid which Septimius concocted, have I been able to learn about it,—its aspect, its properties; and now I suppose it to be quite perfect, and that nothing remains but to put it to such use as he had so long been laboring for. But this, somehow or other, he found in himself a strong reluctance to do; he paused, as it were, at the point where his pathway separated itself from that of other men, and meditated whether it were worth while to give up everything that Providence had provided, and take instead only this lonely gift of immortal life. Not that he ever really had any doubt about it; no, indeed; but it was his security, his consciousness that he held the bright sphere of all futurity in his hand, that made him dally a little, now that he could quaff immortality as soon as he liked.

Besides, now that he looked forward from the verge of mortal destiny, the path before him seemed so very lonely. Might he not seek some one own friend–one single heart–before he took the final step? There was Sibyl Dacy! Oh, what bliss, if that pale girl might set out with him on his journey! how sweet, how sweet, to wander with her through the places else so desolate! for he could but half see, half know things, without her to help him. And perhaps it might be so. She must already know, or strongly suspect, that he was engaged in some deep, mysterious research; it might be that, with her sources of mysterious knowledge among her legendary lore, she knew of this. Then, oh, to think of those dreams which lovers have always had, when their new love makes the old earth seem so happy and glorious a place, that not a thousand nor an endless succession of years can exhaust it,–all those realized for him and her! If this could not be, what should he do? Would he venture onward into such a wintry futurity, symbolized, perhaps, by the coldness of the crystal goblet? He shivered at the thought.

Now, what had passed between Septimius and Sibyl Dacy is not upon record, only that one day they were walking together on the hill-top, or sitting by the little hillock, and talking earnestly together. Sibyl's face was a little flushed with some excitement, and really she looked very beautiful; and Septimius's dark face, too, had a solemn triumph in it that made him also beautiful; so rapt he was after all those watchings, and emaciations, and the pure, unworldly, self-denying life that he had spent. They talked as if there were some foregone conclusion on which they based what they said.

"Will you not be weary in the time that we shall spend together?" asked he.

"Oh no," said Sibyl, smiling, "I am sure that it will be very full of enjoyment."

"Yes," said Septimius, "though now I must remould my anticipations; for I have only dared, hitherto, to map out a solitary existence."

"And how did you do that?" asked Sibyl.

"Oh, there is nothing that would come amiss," answered Septimius; "for, truly, as I have lived apart from men, yet it is really not because I have no taste for whatever humanity includes: but I would fain, if I might, live everybody's life at once, or, since that may not be, each in succession. I would try the life of power, ruling men; but that might come later, after I had had long experience of men, and had lived through much history, and had seen, as a disinterested observer, how men might best be influenced for their own good. I would be a great traveller at first; and as a man newly coming into possession of an estate goes over it, and views each separate field and wood-lot, and whatever features it contains, so will I, whose the world is, because I possess it forever; whereas all others are but transitory guests. So will I wander over this world of mine, and be acquainted with all its shores, seas, rivers, mountains, fields, and the various peoples who inhabit them, and to whom it is my purpose to be a benefactor; for think not, dear Sibyl, that I suppose this great lot of mine to have devolved upon me without great duties,—heavy and difficult to fulfil, though glorious in their adequate fulfilment. But for all this there will be time. In a century I shall partially have seen this earth, and known at least its boundaries,—have gotten for myself the outline, to be filled up hereafter."

"And I, too," said Sibyl, "will have my duties and labors; for while you are wandering about among men, I will go among women, and observe and converse with them, from the princess to the peasant-girl; and will find out what is the matter, that woman gets so large a share of human misery laid on her weak shoulders. I will see why it is that, whether she be a royal princess, she has to be sacrificed to matters of state, or a cottage-girl, still somehow the thing not fit for her is done; and whether there is or no some deadly curse on woman, so that she has nothing to do, and nothing to enjoy, but only to be wronged by man and still to love him, and despise herself for it,—to be shaky in her revenges. And then if, after all this investigation, it turns out—as I suspect—that woman is not capable of being helped, that there is something inherent in herself that makes it hopeless to struggle for her redemption, then what shall I do? Nay, I know not, unless to preach to the sisterhood

145

that they all kill their female children as fast as they are born, and then let the generations of men manage as they can! Woman, so feeble and crazy in body, fair enough sometimes, but full of infirmities; not strong, with nerves prone to every pain; ailing, full of little weaknesses, more contemptible than great ones!"

"That would be a dreary end, Sibyl," said Septimius. "But I trust that we shall be able to hush up this weary and perpetual wail of womankind on easier terms than that. Well, dearest Sibyl, after we have spent a hundred years in examining into the real state of mankind, and another century in devising and putting in execution remedies for his ills, until our maturer thought has time to perfect his cure, we shall then have earned a little playtime,—a century of pastime, in which we will search out whatever joy can be had by thoughtful people, and that childlike sportiveness which comes out of growing wisdom, and enjoyment of every kind. We will gather about us everything beautiful and stately, a great palace, for we shall then be so experienced that all riches will be easy for us to get; with rich furniture, pictures, statues, and all royal ornaments; and side by side with this life we will have a little cottage, and see which is the happiest, for this has always been a dispute. For this century we will neither toil nor spin, nor think of anything beyond the day that is passing over us. There is time enough to do all that we have to do."

"A hundred years of play! Will not that be tiresome?" said Sibyl.

"If it is," said Septimius, "the next century shall make up for it; for then we will contrive deep philosophies, take up one theory after another, and find out its hollowness and inadequacy, and fling it aside, the rotten rubbish that they all are, until we have strewn the whole realm of human thought with the broken fragments, all smashed up. And then, on this great mound of broken potsherds (like that great Monte Testaccio, which we will go to Rome to see), we will build a system that shall stand, and by which mankind shall look far into the ways of Providence, and find practical uses of the deepest kind in what it has thought merely speculation. And then, when the hundred years are over, and this great work done, we will still be so free in mind, that we shall see the emptiness of our own theory, though men see only its truth. And so, if we like more of this pastime, then shall another and another century, and as many more as we like, be spent in the same way."

"And after that another play-day?" asked Sibyl Dacy.

"Yes," said Septimius, "only it shall not be called so; for the next century we will get ourselves made rulers of the earth; and knowing men so well, and having so wrought our theories of government and what not, we will proceed to execute them,–which will be as easy to us as a child's arrangement of its dolls. We will smile superior, to see what a facile thing it is to make a people happy. In our reign of a hundred years, we shall have time to extinguish errors, and make the world see the absurdity of them; to substitute other methods of government for the old, bad ones; to fit the people to govern itself, to do with little government, to do with none; and when this is effected, we will vanish from our loving people, and be seen no more, but be reverenced as gods,–we, meanwhile, being overlooked, and smiling to ourselves, amid the very crowd that is looking for us."

"I intend," said Sibyl, making this wild talk wilder by that petulance which she so often showed,–"I intend to introduce a new fashion of dress when I am queen, and that shall be my part of the great reform which you are going to make. And for my crown, I intend to have it of flowers, in which that strange crimson one shall be the chief; and when I vanish, this flower shall remain behind, and perhaps they shall have a glimpse of me wearing it in the crowd. Well, what next?"

"After this," said Septimius, "having seen so much of affairs, and having lived so many hundred years, I will sit down and write a history, such as histories ought to be, and never have been. And it shall be so wise, and so vivid, and so self-evidently true, that people shall be convinced from it that there is some undying one among them, because only an eye-witness could have written it, or could have gained so much wisdom as was needful for it."

"And for my part in the history," said Sibyl, "I will record the various lengths of women's waists, and the fashion of their sleeves. What next?"

"By this time," said Septimius,–"how many hundred years have we now lived?–by this time, I shall have pretty well prepared myself for what I have been contemplating from the first. I will become a religious teacher, and promulgate a faith, and prove it by prophecies and miracles; for my long experience will enable me to do the first, and the acquaintance which I shall have formed with the mysteries of science will put the latter at my fingers' ends. So I will be a prophet, a greater than Mahomet, and will put all man's hopes into my doctrine, and make him good, holy, happy; and he shall put up his prayers to his Creator, and find them answered, because they shall be wise, and accompanied with effort. This will be a great work, and may earn me another rest and pastime."

[He would see, in one age, the column raised in memory of some great dead of his in a former one.]

"And what shall that be?" asked Sibyl Dacy.

"Why," said Septimius, looking askance at her, and speaking with a certain hesitation, "I have learned, Sibyl, that it is a weary toil for a man to be always good, holy, and upright. In my life as a sainted prophet, I shall have somewhat too much of this; it will be enervating and sickening, and I shall need another kind of diet. So, in the next hundred years, Sibyl,–in that one little century,–methinks I would fain be what men call wicked. How can I know my brethren, unless I do that once? I would experience all. Imagination is only a dream. I can imagine myself a murderer, and all other modes of crime; but it leaves no real impression on the heart. I must live these things."

[The rampant unrestraint, which is the characteristic of wickedness.]

"Good," said Sibyl, quietly; "and I too."

"And thou too!" exclaimed Septimius. "Not so, Sibyl. I would reserve thee, good and pure, so that there may be to me the means of redemption,– some stable hold in the moral confusion that I will create around myself, whereby I shall by and by get back into order, virtue, and religion. Else all is lost, and I may become a devil, and make my own hell around me; so, Sibyl, do thou be good forever, and not fall nor slip a moment. Promise me!"

"We will consider about that in some other century," replied Sibyl, composedly. "There is time enough yet. What next?"

"Nay, this is enough for the present," said Septimius. "New vistas will open themselves before us continually, as we go onward. How idle to think that one little lifetime would exhaust the world! After hundreds of centuries, I feel as if we might still be on the threshold. There is the material world, for instance, to perfect; to draw out the powers of nature, so that man shall, as it were, give life to all modes of matter, and make them his ministering servants. Swift ways of travel, by earth, sea, and air; machines for doing whatever the hand of man now does, so that we shall do all but put souls into our wheel-work and watch-work; the modes of making night into day; of getting control over the weather and the seasons; the virtues of plants,–these are some of the easier things thou shalt help me do."

"I have no taste for that," said Sibyl, "unless I could make an embroidery worked of steel."

"And so, Sibyl," continued Septimius, pursuing his strain of solemn enthusiasm, intermingled as it was with wild, excursive vagaries, "we will go on as many centuries as we choose. Perhaps,–yet I think not so,–perhaps, however, in the course of lengthened time, we may find that the world is the same always, and mankind the same, and all possibilities of human fortune the same; so that by and by we shall discover that the same old scenery serves the world's stage in all ages, and that the story is always the same; yes, and the actors always the same, though none but we can be aware of it; and that the actors and spectators would grow weary of it, were they not bathed in forgetful sleep, and so think themselves new made in each successive lifetime. We may find that the stuff of the world's drama, and the passions which seem to play in it, have a monotony, when once we have tried them; that in only once trying them, and viewing them, we find out their secret, and that afterwards the show is too superficial to arrest our attention. As dramatists and novelists repeat their plots, so does man's life repeat itself, and at length grows stale. This is what, in my desponding moments, I have sometimes suspected. What to do, if this be so?"

"Nay, that is a serious consideration," replied Sibyl, assuming an air of mock alarm, "if you really think we shall be tired of life, whether or no."

"I do not think it, Sibyl," replied Septimius. "By much musing on this matter, I have convinced myself that man is not capable of debarring himself utterly from death, since it is evidently a remedy for many evils that nothing else would cure. This means that we have discovered of removing death to an indefinite distance is not supernatural; on the contrary, it is the most natural thing in the world,—the very perfection of the natural, since it consists in applying the powers and processes of Nature to the prolongation of the existence of man, her most perfect handiwork; and this could only be done by entire accordance and co-effort with Nature. Therefore Nature is not changed, and death remains as one of her steps, just as heretofore. Therefore, when we have exhausted the world, whether by going through its apparently vast variety, or by satisfying ourselves that it is all a repetition of one thing, we will call death as the friend to introduce us to something new."

[He would write a poem, or other great work, inappreciable at first, and live to see it famous,—himself among his own posterity.]

"Oh, insatiable love of life!" exclaimed Sibyl, looking at him with strange pity. "Canst thou not conceive that mortal brain and heart might at length be content to sleep?"

"Never, Sibyl!" replied Septimius, with horror. "My spirit delights in the thought of an infinite eternity. Does not thine?"

"One little interval—a few centuries only—of dreamless sleep," said Sibyl, pleadingly. "Cannot you allow me that?"

"I fear," said Septimius, "our identity would change in that repose; it would be a Lethe between the two parts of our being, and with such disconnection a continued life would be equivalent to a new one, and therefore valueless."

In such talk, snatching in the fog at the fragments of philosophy, they continued fitfully; Septimius calming down his enthusiasm thus, which otherwise might have burst forth in madness, affrighting the quiet little village with the marvellous things about which they mused. Septimius could not quite satisfy himself whether Sibyl Dacy shared in his belief of the success of his experiment, and was confident, as he was, that he held in his control the means of unlimited life; neither was he sure that she loved him,–loved him well enough to undertake with him the long march that he propounded to her, making a union an affair of so vastly more importance than it is in the brief lifetime of other mortals. But he determined to let her drink the invaluable draught along with him, and to trust to the long future, and the better opportunities that time would give him, and his outliving all rivals, and the loneliness which an undying life would throw around her, without him, as the pledges of his success.

And now the happy day had come for the celebration of Robert Hagburn's marriage with pretty Rose Garfield, the brave with the fair; and, as usual, the ceremony was to take place in the evening, and at the house of the bride; and preparations were made accordingly: the wedding-cake, which the bride's own fair hands had mingled with her tender hopes, and seasoned it with maiden fears, so that its composition was as much ethereal as sensual; and the neighbors and friends were invited, and came with their best wishes and good-will. For Rose shared not at all the distrust, the suspicion, or whatever it was, that had waited on the true branch of Septimius's family, in one shape or another, ever since the memory of man; and all–except, it might be, some disappointed damsels who had hoped to win Robert Hagburn for themselves–rejoiced at the approaching union of this fit couple, and wished them happiness.

Septimius, too, accorded his gracious consent to the union, and while he thought within himself that such a brief union was not worth the trouble and feeling which his sister and her lover wasted on it, still he wished them happiness. As he compared their brevity with his long duration, he smiled at their little fancies of loves, of which he seemed to see the end; the flower of a brief summer, blooming beautifully enough, and shedding its leaves, the fragrance of which would linger a little while in his memory, and then be gone. He wondered how far in the coming centuries he should remember this wedding of his sister Rose; perhaps he would meet, five hundred years hence, some descendant of the marriage,–a fair girl, bearing the traits of his sister's fresh beauty; a young man, recalling the strength and manly comeliness of Robert Hagburn,–and could claim acquaintance and kindred. He would be the guardian, from generation to generation, of this race; their ever-reappearing friend at times of need; and meeting them from age to age, would find traditions of himself growing poetical in the lapse of time; so that he would smile at seeing his features look so much more majestic in their fancies than in reality. So all along their course, in the history of the family, he would trace himself, and by his traditions he would make them acquainted with all their ancestors, and so still be warmed by kindred blood.

And Robert Hagburn, full of the life of the moment, warm with generous blood, came in a new uniform, looking fit to be the founder of a race who should look back to a hero sire. He greeted Septimius as a brother. The minister, too, came, of course, and mingled with the throng, with decorous aspect, and greeted Septimius with more formality than he had been wont; for Septimius had insensibly withdrawn himself from the minister's intimacy, as he got deeper and deeper into the enthusiasm of his own cause. Besides, the minister did not fail to see that his once devoted scholar had contracted habits of study into the secrets of which he himself was not admitted, and that he no longer alluded to studies for the ministry; and he was inclined to suspect that Septimius had unfortunately allowed infidel ideas to assail, at least, if not to overcome, that fortress of firm faith, which he had striven to found and strengthen in his mind,–a misfortune frequently befalling speculative and imaginative and melancholic persons, like Septimius, whom the Devil is all the time planning to assault, because he feels confident of having a traitor in the garrison. The minister had heard that this was the fashion of Septimius's family, and that even the famous divine, who, in his eyes, was the glory of it, had had his season of wild infidelity in his youth, before grace touched him; and had always thereafter, throughout his long and pious life, been subject to seasons of black and sulphurous despondency, during which he disbelieved the faith which, at other times, he preached powerfully."

"Septimius, my young friend," said he, "are you yet ready to be a preacher of the truth?"

"Not yet, reverend pastor," said Septimius, smiling at the thought of the day before, that the career of a prophet would be one that he should some time assume. "There will be time enough to preach the truth when I better know it."

"You do not look as if you knew it so well as formerly, instead of better," said his reverend friend, looking into the deep furrows of his brow, and into his wild and troubled eyes.

"Perhaps not," said Septimius. "There is time yet."

These few words passed amid the bustle and murmur of the evening, while the guests were assembling, and all were awaiting the marriage with that interest which the event continually brings with it, common as it is, so that nothing but death is commoner. Everybody congratulated the modest Rose, who looked quiet and happy; and so she stood up at the proper time, and the minister married them with a certain fervor and individual application, that made them feel they were married indeed. Then there ensued a salutation of the bride, the first to kiss her being the minister, and then some respectable old justices and farmers, each with his friendly smile and joke. Then went round the cake and wine, and other good cheer, and the hereditary jokes with which brides used to be assailed in those days. I think, too, there was a dance, though how the couples in the reel found space to foot it in the little room, I cannot imagine; at any rate, there was a bright light out of the windows, gleaming across the road, and such a sound of the babble of numerous voices and merriment, that travellers passing by, on the lonely Lexington road, wished they were of the party; and one or two of them stopped and went in, and saw the new-made bride, drank to her health, and took a piece of the wedding-cake home to dream upon.

[It is to be observed that Rose had requested of her friend, Sibyl Dacy, to act as one of her bridesmaids, of whom she had only the modest number of two; and the strange girl declined, saying that her intermeddling would bring ill-fortune to the marriage.]

"Why do you talk such nonsense, Sibyl?" asked Rose. "You love me, I am sure, and wish me well; and your smile, such as it is, will be the promise of prosperity, and I wish for it on my wedding-day."

"I am an ill-fate, a sinister demon, Rose; a thing that has sprung out of a grave; and you had better not entreat me to twine my poison tendrils round your destinies. You would repent it."

"Oh, hush, hush!" said Rose, putting her hand over her friend's mouth. "Naughty one! you can bless me, if you will, only you are wayward."

"Bless you, then, dearest Rose, and all happiness on your marriage!"

Septimius had been duly present at the marriage, and kissed his sister with moist eyes, it is said, and a solemn smile, as he gave her into the keeping of Robert Hagburn; and there was something in the words he then used that afterwards dwelt on her mind, as if they had a meaning in them that asked to be sought into, and needed reply.

"There, Rose," he had said, "I have made myself ready for my destiny. I have no ties any more, and may set forth on my path without scruple."

"Am I not your sister still, Septimius?" said she, shedding a tear or two.

"A married woman is no sister; nothing but a married woman till she becomes a mother; and then what shall I have to do with you?"

He spoke with a certain eagerness to prove his case, which Rose could not understand, but which was probably to justify himself in severing, as he was about to do, the link that connected him with his race, and making for himself an exceptional destiny, which, if it did not entirely insulate him, would at least create new relations with all. There he stood, poor fellow, looking on the mirthful throng, not in exultation, as might have been supposed, but with a strange sadness upon him. It seemed to him, at that final moment, as if it were Death that linked together all; yes, and so gave the warmth to all. Wedlock itself seemed a brother of Death; wedlock, and its sweetest hopes, its holy companionship, its mysteries, and all that warm mysterious brotherhood that is between men; passing as they do from mystery to mystery in a little gleam of light; that wild, sweet charm of uncertainty and temporariness,—how lovely it made them all, how innocent, even the worst of them; how hard and prosaic was his own situation in comparison to theirs. He felt a gushing tenderness for them, as if he would have flung aside his endless life, and rushed among them, saying,—

154

"Embrace me! I am still one of you, and will not leave you! Hold me fast!"

After this it was not particularly observed that both Septimius and Sibyl Dacy had disappeared from the party, which, however, went on no less merrily without them. In truth, the habits of Sibyl Dacy were so wayward, and little squared by general rules, that nobody wondered or tried to account for them; and as for Septimius, he was such a studious man, so little accustomed to mingle with his fellow-citizens on any occasion, that it was rather wondered at that he should have spent so large a part of a sociable evening with them, than that he should now retire.

After they were gone the party received an unexpected addition, being no other than the excellent Doctor Portsoaken, who came to the door, announcing that he had just arrived on horseback from Boston, and that, his object being to have an interview with Sibyl Dacy, he had been to Robert Hagburn's house in quest of her; but, learning from the old grandmother that she was here, he had followed.

Not finding her, he evinced no alarm, but was easily induced to sit down among the merry company, and partake of some brandy, which, with other liquors, Robert had provided in sufficient abundance; and that being a day when man had not learned to fear the glass, the doctor found them all in a state of hilarious chat. Taking out his German pipe, he joined the group of smokers in the great chimney-corner, and entered into conversation with them, laughing and joking, and mixing up his jests with that mysterious suspicion which gave so strange a character to his intercourse.

"It is good fortune, Mr. Hagburn," quoth he, "that brings me here on this auspicious day. And how has been my learned young friend Dr. Septimius,– for so he should be called,–and how have flourished his studies of late? The scientific world may look for great fruits from that decoction of his."

"He'll never equal Aunt Keziah for herb-drinks," said an old woman, smoking her pipe in the corner, "though I think likely he'll make a good doctor enough by and by. Poor Kezzy, she took a drop too much of her mixture, after all. I used to tell her how it would be; for Kezzy and I were pretty good friends once, before the Indian in her came out so strongly,—the squaw and the witch, for she had them both in her blood, poor yellow Kezzy!"

"Yes! had she indeed?" quoth the doctor; "and I have heard an odd story, that if the Feltons chose to go back to the old country, they'd find a home and an estate there ready for them."

The old woman mused, and puffed at her pipe. "Ah, yes," muttered she, at length, "I remember to have heard something about that; and how, if Felton chose to strike into the woods, he'd find a tribe of wild Indians there ready to take him for their sagamore, and conquer the whites; and how, if he chose to go to England, there was a great old house all ready for him, and a fire burning in the hall, and a dinner-table spread, and the tall-posted bed ready, with clean sheets, in the best chamber, and a man waiting at the gate to show him in. Only there was a spell of a bloody footstep left on the threshold by the last that came out, so that none of his posterity could ever cross it again. But that was all nonsense!"

"Strange old things one dreams in a chimney-corner," quoth the doctor. "Do you remember any more of this?"

"No, no; I'm so forgetful nowadays," said old Mrs. Hagburn; "only it seems as if I had my memories in my pipe, and they curl up in smoke. I've known these Feltons all along, or it seems as if I had; for I'm nigh ninety years old now, and I was two year old in the witch's time, and I have seen a piece of the halter that old Felton was hung with."

Some of the company laughed.

"That must have been a curious sight," quoth the doctor.

"It is not well," said the minister seriously to the doctor, "to stir up these old remembrances, making the poor old lady appear absurd. I know not that she need to be ashamed of showing the weaknesses of the generation to which she belonged; but I do not like to see old age put at this disadvantage among the young."

156

"Nay, my good and reverend sir," returned the doctor, "I mean no such disrespect as you seem to think. Forbid it, ye upper powers, that I should cast any ridicule on beliefs,–superstitions, do you call them?–that are as worthy of faith, for aught I know, as any that are preached in the pulpit. If the old lady would tell me any secret of the old Felton's science, I shall treasure it sacredly; for I interpret these stories about his miraculous gifts as meaning that he had a great command over natural science, the virtues of plants, the capacities of the human body."

"While these things were passing, or before they passed, or some time in that eventful night, Septimius had withdrawn to his study, when there was a low tap at the door, and, opening it, Sibyl Dacy stood before him. It seemed as if there had been a previous arrangement between them; for Septimius evinced no surprise, only took her hand and drew her in.

"How cold your hand is!" he exclaimed. "Nothing is so cold, except it be the potent medicine. It makes me shiver."

"Never mind that," said Sibyl. "You look frightened at me."

"Do I?" said Septimius. "No, not that; but this is such a crisis; and methinks it is not yourself. Your eyes glare on me strangely."

"Ah, yes; and you are not frightened at me? Well, I will try not to be frightened at myself. Time was, however, when I should have been."

She looked round at Septimius's study, with its few old books, its implements of science, crucibles, retorts, and electrical machines; all these she noticed little; but on the table drawn before the fire, there was something that attracted her attention; it was a vase that seemed of crystal, made in that old fashion in which the Venetians made their glasses,–a most pure kind of glass, with a long stalk, within which was a curved elaboration of fancy-work, wreathed and twisted. This old glass was an heirloom of the Feltons, a relic that had come down with many traditions, bringing its frail fabric safely through all the perils of time, that had shattered empires; and, if space sufficed, I could tell many stories of this curious vase, which was said, in its time, to have been the instrument both of the Devil's sacrament in the forest,

157

and of the Christian in the village meeting-house. But, at any rate, it had been a part of the choice household gear of one of Septimius's ancestors, and was engraved with his arms, artistically done.

"Is that the drink of immortality?" said Sibyl.

"Yes, Sibyl," said Septimius. "Do but touch the goblet; see how cold it is."

She put her slender, pallid fingers on the side of the goblet, and shuddered, just as Septimius did when he touched her hand.

"Why should it be so cold?" said she, looking at Septimius.

"Nay, I know not, unless because endless life goes round the circle and meets death, and is just the same with it. O Sibyl, it is a fearful thing that I have accomplished! Do you not feel it so? What if this shiver should last us through eternity?"

"Have you pursued this object so long," said Sibyl, "to have these fears respecting it now? In that case, methinks I could be bold enough to drink it alone, and look down upon you, as I did so, smiling at your fear to take the life offered you."

"I do not fear," said Septimius; "but yet I acknowledge there is a strange, powerful abhorrence in me towards this draught, which I know not how to account for, except as the reaction, the revulsion of feeling, consequent upon its being too long overstrained in one direction. I cannot help it. The meannesses, the littlenesses, the perplexities, the general irksomeness of life, weigh upon me strangely. Thou didst refuse to drink with me. That being the case, methinks I could break the jewelled goblet now, untasted, and choose the grave as the wiser part."

"The beautiful goblet! What a pity to break it!" said Sibyl, with her characteristic malign and mysterious smile. "You cannot find it in your heart to do it."

"I could,—I can. So thou wilt not drink with me?"

"Do you know what you ask?" said Sibyl. "I am a being that sprung up, like this flower, out of a grave; or, at least, I took root in a grave, and, growing there, have twined about your life, until you cannot possibly escape from me. Ah, Septimius! you know me not. You know not what is in my heart towards you. Do you remember this broken miniature? would you wish to see the features that were destroyed when that bullet passed? Then look at mine!"

"Sibyl! what do you tell me? Was it you—were they your features—which that young soldier kissed as he lay dying?"

"They were," said Sibyl. "I loved him, and gave him that miniature, and the face they represented. I had given him all, and you slew him."

"Then you hate me," whispered, Septimius.

"Do you call it hatred?" asked Sibyl, smiling. "Have I not aided you, thought with you, encouraged you, heard all your wild ravings when you dared to tell no one else? kept up your hopes; suggested; helped you with my legendary lore to useful hints; helped you, also, in other ways, which you do not suspect? And now you ask me if I hate you. Does this look like it?"

"No," said Septimius. "And yet, since first I knew you, there has been something whispering me of harm, as if I sat near some mischief. There is in me the wild, natural blood of the Indian, the instinctive, the animal nature, which has ways of warning that civilized life polishes away and cuts out; and so, Sibyl, never did I approach you, but there were reluctances, drawings back, and, at the same time, a strong impulse to come closest to you; and to that I yielded. But why, then, knowing that in this grave lay the man you loved, laid there by my hand,—why did you aid me in an object which you must have seen was the breath of my life?"

"Ah, my friend,—my enemy, if you will have it so,—are you yet to learn that the wish of a man's inmost heart is oftenest that by which he is ruined and made miserable? But listen to me, Septimius. No matter for my earlier life; there is no reason why I should tell you the story, and confess to you its weakness, its shame. It may be, I had more cause to hate the tenant of that grave, than to hate you who unconsciously avenged my cause; nevertheless, I came here in hatred, and desire of revenge, meaning to lie in wait, and turn your dearest desire against you, to eat into your life, and distil poison into it, I sitting on this grave, and drawing fresh hatred from it; and at last, in the hour of your triumph, I meant to make the triumph mine."

"Is this still so?" asked Septimius, with pale lips: "or did your fell purpose change?"

"Septimius, I am weak,–a weak, weak girl,–only a girl, Septimius; only eighteen yet," exclaimed Sibyl. "It is young, is it not? I might be forgiven much. You know not how bitter my purpose was to you. But look, Septimius,–could it be worse than this? Hush, be still! Do not stir!"

She lifted the beautiful goblet from the table, put it to her lips, and drank a deep draught from it; then, smiling mockingly, she held it towards him.

"See; I have made myself immortal before you. Will you drink?"

He eagerly held out his hand to receive the goblet, but Sibyl, holding it beyond his reach a moment, deliberately let it fall upon the hearth, where it shivered into fragments, and the bright, cold water of immortality was all spilt, shedding its strange fragrance around.

"Sibyl, what have you done?" cried Septimius in rage and horror.

"Be quiet! See what sort of immortality I win by it,–then, if you like, distil your drink of eternity again, and quaff it."

"It is too late, Sibyl; it was a happiness that may never come again in a lifetime. I shall perish as a dog does. It is too late!"

"Septimius," said Sibyl, who looked strangely beautiful, as if the drink, giving her immortal life, had likewise the potency to give immortal beauty answering to it, "listen to me. You have not learned all the secrets that lay in those old legends, about which we have talked so much. There were two recipes, discovered or learned by the art of the studious old Gaspar Felton. One was said to be that secret of immortal life which so many old sages sought for, and which some were said to have found; though, if that were the case, it is strange some of them have not lived till our day. Its essence lay in a certain rare flower, which mingled properly with other ingredients of great potency in themselves, though still lacking the crowning virtue till the flower was supplied, produced the drink of immortality."

"Yes, and I had the flower, which I found in a grave," said Septimius, "and distilled the drink which you have spilt."

"You had a flower, or what you called a flower," said the girl. "But, Septimius, there was yet another drink, in which the same potent ingredients were used; all but the last. In this, instead of the beautiful flower, was mingled the semblance of a flower, but really a baneful growth out of a grave. This I sowed there, and it converted the drink into a poison, famous in old science,–a poison which the Borgias used, and Mary de Medicis,–and which has brought to death many a famous person, when it was desirable to his enemies. This is the drink I helped you to distil. It brings on death with pleasant and delightful thrills of the nerves. O Septimius, Septimius, it is worth while to die, to be so blest, so exhilarated as I am now."

"Good God, Sibyl, is this possible?"

"Even so, Septimius. I was helped by that old physician, Doctor Portsoaken, who, with some private purpose of his own, taught me what to do; for he was skilled in all the mysteries of those old physicians, and knew that their poisons at least were efficacious, whatever their drinks of immortality might be. But the end has not turned out as I meant. A girl's fancy is so shifting, Septimius. I thought I loved that youth in the grave yonder; but it was you I loved,–and I am dying. Forgive me for my evil purposes, for I am dying."

"Why hast thou spilt the drink?" said Septimius, bending his dark brows upon her, and frowning over her. "We might have died together."

"No, live, Septimius," said the girl, whose face appeared to grow bright and joyous, as if the drink of death exhilarated her like an intoxicating fluid. "I would not let you have it, not one drop. But to think," and here she laughed, "what a penance,–what months of wearisome labor thou hast had,–and what thoughts, what dreams, and how I laughed in my sleeve at them all the time! Ha, ha, ha! Then thou didst plan out future ages, and talk poetry and prose to me. Did I not take it very demurely, and answer thee in the same style? and so thou didst love me, and kindly didst wish to take me with thee in thy immortality. O Septimius, I should have liked it well! Yes, latterly, only, I knew how the case stood. Oh, how I surrounded thee with dreams, and instead of giving thee immortal life, so kneaded up the little life allotted thee with dreams and vaporing stuff, that thou didst not really live even that. Ah, it was a pleasant pastime, and pleasant is now the end of it. Kiss me, thou poor Septimius, one kiss!"

[She gives the ridiculous aspect to his scheme, in an airy way.]

But as Septimius, who seemed stunned, instinctively bent forward to obey her, she drew back. "No, there shall be no kiss! There may a little poison linger on my lips. Farewell! Dost thou mean still to seek for thy liquor of immortality?–ah, ah! It was a good jest. We will laugh at it when we meet in the other world."

And here poor Sibyl Dacy's laugh grew fainter, and dying away, she seemed to die with it; for there she was, with that mirthful, half-malign expression still on her face, but motionless; so that however long Septimius's life was likely to be, whether a few years or many centuries, he would still have her image in his memory so. And here she lay among his broken hopes, now shattered as completely as the goblet which held his draught, and as incapable of being formed again.

The next day, as Septimius did not appear, there was research for him on the part of Doctor Portsoaken. His room was found empty, the bed untouched. Then they sought him on his favorite hill-top; but neither was he found there, although something was found that added to the wonder and alarm of his disappearance. It was the cold form of Sibyl Dacy, which was extended on the hillock so often mentioned, with her arms thrown over it; but, looking in the dead face, the beholders were astonished to see a certain malign and mirthful expression, as if some airy part had been played out,–

some surprise, some practical joke of a peculiarly airy kind had burst with fairy shoots of fire among the company.

"Ah, she is dead! Poor Sibyl Dacy!" exclaimed Doctor Portsoaken. "Her scheme, then, has turned out amiss."

This exclamation seemed to imply some knowledge of the mystery; and it so impressed the auditors, among whom was Robert Hagburn, that they thought it not inexpedient to have an investigation; so the learned doctor was not uncivilly taken into custody and examined. Several interesting particulars, some of which throw a certain degree of light on our narrative, were discovered. For instance, that Sibyl Dacy, who was a niece of the doctor, had been beguiled from her home and led over the sea by Cyril Norton, and that the doctor, arriving in Boston with another regiment, had found her there, after her lover's death. Here there was some discrepancy or darkness in the doctor's narrative. He appeared to have consented to, or instigated (for it was not quite evident how far his concurrence had gone) this poor girl's scheme of going and brooding over her lover's grave, and living in close contiguity with the man who had slain him. The doctor had not much to say for himself on this point; but there was found reason to believe that he was acting in the interest of some English claimant of a great estate that was left without an apparent heir by the death of Cyril Norton, and there was even a suspicion that he, with his fantastic science and antiquated empiricism, had been at the bottom of the scheme of poisoning, which was so strangely intertwined with Septimius's notion, in which he went so nearly crazed, of a drink of immortality. It was observable, however, that the doctor–such a humbug in scientific matters, that he had perhaps bewildered himself–seemed to have a sort of faith in the efficacy of the recipe which had so strangely come to light, provided the true flower could be discovered; but that flower, according to Doctor Portsoaken, had not been seen on earth for many centuries, and was banished probably forever. The flower, or fungus, which Septimius had mistaken for it, was a sort of earthly or devilish counterpart of it, and was greatly in request among the old poisoners for its admirable uses in their art. In fine, no tangible evidence being found against the worthy doctor, he was permitted to depart, and disappeared from the neighborhood, to the scandal of many people, unhanged; leaving behind him few available effects beyond the web and empty skin of an enormous spider.

As to Septimius, he returned no more to his cottage by the wayside, and none undertook to tell what had become of him; crushed and annihilated, as it were, by the failure of his magnificent and most absurd dreams. Rumors there have been, however, at various times, that there had appeared an American claimant, who had made out his right to the great estate of Smithell's Hall, and had dwelt there, and left posterity, and that in the subsequent generation an ancient baronial title had been revived in favor of the son and heir of the American. Whether this was our Septimius, I cannot tell; but I should be rather sorry to believe that after such splendid schemes as he had entertained, he should have been content to settle down into the fat substance and reality of English life, and die in his due time, and be buried like any other man.

A few years ago, while in England, I visited Smithell's Hall, and was entertained there, not knowing at the time that I could claim its owner as my countryman by descent; though, as I now remember, I was struck by the thin, sallow, American cast of his face, and the lithe slenderness of his figure, and seem now (but this may be my fancy) to recollect a certain Indian glitter of the eye and cast of feature.

As for the Bloody Footstep, I saw it with my own eyes, and will venture to suggest that it was a mere natural reddish stain in the stone, converted by superstition into a Bloody Footstep.

About Author

Nathaniel Hawthorne (**Hathorne**; July 4, 1804 – May 19, 1864) was an American novelist, dark romantic, and short story writer. His works often focus on history, morality, and religion.

He was born in 1804 in Salem, Massachusetts, to Nathaniel Hathorne and the former Elizabeth Clarke Manning. His ancestors include John Hathorne, the only judge involved in the Salem witch trials who never repented of his actions. He entered Bowdoin College in 1821, was elected to Phi Beta Kappa in 1824, and graduated in 1825. He published his first work in 1828, the novel Fanshawe; he later tried to suppress it, feeling that it was not equal to the standard of his later work. He published several short stories in periodicals, which he collected in 1837 as Twice-Told Tales. The next year, he became engaged to Sophia Peabody. He worked at the Boston Custom House and joined Brook Farm, a transcendentalist community, before marrying Peabody in 1842. The couple moved to The Old Manse in Concord, Massachusetts, later moving to Salem, the Berkshires, then to The Wayside in Concord. The Scarlet Letter was published in 1850, followed by a succession of other novels. A political appointment as consul took Hawthorne and family to Europe before their return to Concord in 1860. Hawthorne died on May 19, 1864, and was survived by his wife and their three children.

Much of Hawthorne's writing centers on New England, many works featuring moral metaphors with an anti-Puritan inspiration. His fiction works are considered part of the Romantic movement and, more specifically, dark romanticism. His themes often center on the inherent evil and sin of humanity, and his works often have moral messages and deep psychological complexity. His published works include novels, short stories, and a biography of his college friend Franklin Pierce, the 14th President of the United States.

Biography

Early life

Nathaniel Hawthorne was born on July 4, 1804, in Salem, Massachusetts;

his birthplace is preserved and open to the public. William Hathorne was the author's great-great-great-grandfather. He was a Puritan and was the first of the family to emigrate from England, settling in Dorchester, Massachusetts, before moving to Salem. There he became an important member of the Massachusetts Bay Colony and held many political positions, including magistrate and judge, becoming infamous for his harsh sentencing. William's son and the author's great-great-grandfather John Hathorne was one of the judges who oversaw the Salem witch trials. Hawthorne probably added the "w" to his surname in his early twenties, shortly after graduating from college, in an effort to dissociate himself from his notorious forebears. Hawthorne's father Nathaniel Hathorne Sr. was a sea captain who died in 1808 of yellow fever in Suriname; he had been a member of the East India Marine Society. After his death, his widow moved with young Nathaniel and two daughters to live with relatives named the Mannings in Salem, where they lived for 10 years. Young Hawthorne was hit on the leg while playing "bat and ball" on November 10, 1813, and he became lame and bedridden for a year, though several physicians could find nothing wrong with him.

In the summer of 1816, the family lived as boarders with farmers before moving to a home recently built specifically for them by Hawthorne's uncles Richard and Robert Manning in Raymond, Maine, near Sebago Lake. Years later, Hawthorne looked back at his time in Maine fondly: "Those were delightful days, for that part of the country was wild then, with only scattered clearings, and nine tenths of it primeval woods." In 1819, he was sent back to Salem for school and soon complained of homesickness and being too far from his mother and sisters. He distributed seven issues of The Spectator to his family in August and September 1820 for the sake of having fun. The homemade newspaper was written by hand and included essays, poems, and news featuring the young author's adolescent humor.

Hawthorne's uncle Robert Manning insisted that the boy attend college, despite Hawthorne's protests. With the financial support of his uncle, Hawthorne was sent to Bowdoin College in 1821, partly because of family connections in the area, and also because of its relatively inexpensive tuition rate. Hawthorne met future president Franklin Pierce on the way to

Bowdoin, at the stage stop in Portland, and the two became fast friends. Once at the school, he also met future poet Henry Wadsworth Longfellow, future congressman Jonathan Cilley, and future naval reformer Horatio Bridge. He graduated with the class of 1825, and later described his college experience to Richard Henry Stoddard:

> I was educated (as the phrase is) at Bowdoin College. I was an idle student, negligent of college rules and the Procrustean details of academic life, rather choosing to nurse my own fancies than to dig into Greek roots and be numbered among the learned Thebans.

Early career

In 1836, Hawthorne served as the editor of the American Magazine of Useful and Entertaining Knowledge. At the time, he boarded with poet Thomas Green Fessenden on Hancock Street in Beacon Hill in Boston. He was offered an appointment as weigher and gauger at the Boston Custom House at a salary of $1,500 a year, which he accepted on January 17, 1839. During his time there, he rented a room from George Stillman Hillard, business partner of Charles Sumner. Hawthorne wrote in the comparative obscurity of what he called his "owl's nest" in the family home. As he looked back on this period of his life, he wrote: "I have not lived, but only dreamed about living." He contributed short stories to various magazines and annuals, including "Young Goodman Brown" and "The Minister's Black Veil", though none drew major attention to him. Horatio Bridge offered to cover the risk of collecting these stories in the spring of 1837 into the volume Twice-Told Tales, which made Hawthorne known locally.

Marriage and family

While at Bowdoin, Hawthorne wagered a bottle of Madeira wine with his friend Jonathan Cilley that Cilley would get married before Hawthorne did. By 1836, he had won the bet, but he did not remain a bachelor for life. He had public flirtations with Mary Silsbee and Elizabeth Peabody, then he began pursuing Peabody's sister, illustrator and transcendentalist Sophia Peabody. He joined the transcendentalist Utopian community at Brook Farm in 1841, not because he agreed with the experiment but because it helped him save money to marry Sophia. He paid a $1,000 deposit and was put in charge of shoveling the hill of manure referred to as "the Gold Mine". He left later that year, though his Brook Farm adventure became an inspiration for his novel The Blithedale Romance. Hawthorne married Sophia Peabody on July 9, 1842, at a ceremony in the Peabody parlor on West Street in Boston. The couple moved to The Old Manse in Concord, Massachusetts, where they lived for three years. His neighbor Ralph Waldo Emerson invited him into his social circle, but Hawthorne was almost pathologically shy and stayed silent at gatherings. At the Old Manse, Hawthorne wrote most of the tales collected in Mosses from an Old Manse.

Like Hawthorne, Sophia was a reclusive person. Throughout her early life, she had frequent migraines and underwent several experimental medical treatments. She was mostly bedridden until her sister introduced her to Hawthorne, after which her headaches seem to have abated. The Hawthornes enjoyed a long and happy marriage. He referred to her as his "Dove" and wrote that she "is, in the strictest sense, my sole companion; and I need no other—there is no vacancy in my mind, any more than in my heart ... Thank God that I suffice for her boundless heart!" Sophia greatly admired her husband's work. She wrote in one of her journals:

> I am always so dazzled and bewildered with the richness, the depth, the ... jewels of beauty in his productions that I am always looking forward to a second reading where I can ponder and muse and fully take in the miraculous wealth of thoughts.

Poet Ellery Channing came to the Old Manse for help on the first anniversary of the Hawthornes' marriage. A local teenager named Martha Hunt had drowned herself in the river and Hawthorne's boat Pond Lily was needed to find her body. Hawthorne helped recover the corpse, which he described as "a spectacle of such perfect horror ... She was the very image of death-agony". The incident later inspired a scene in his novel The Blithedale Romance.

The Hawthornes had three children. Their first was daughter Una, born March 3, 1844; her name was a reference to The Faerie Queene, to the displeasure of family members. Hawthorne wrote to a friend, "I find it a very sober and serious kind of happiness that springs from the birth of a child ... There is no escaping it any longer. I have business on earth now, and must look about me for the means of doing it." In October 1845, the Hawthornes moved to Salem. In 1846, their son Julian was born. Hawthorne wrote to his sister Louisa on June 22, 1846: "A small troglodyte made his appearance here at ten minutes to six o'clock this morning, who claimed to be your nephew." Daughter Rose was born in May 1851, and Hawthorne called her his "autumnal flower".

Middle years

In April 1846, Hawthorne was officially appointed the Surveyor for the District of Salem and Beverly and Inspector of the Revenue for the Port of Salem at an annual salary of $1,200. He had difficulty writing during this period, as he admitted to Longfellow:

> I am trying to resume my pen ... Whenever I sit alone, or walk alone, I find myself dreaming about stories, as of old; but these forenoons in the Custom House undo all that the afternoons and evenings have done. I should be happier if I could write.

This employment, like his earlier appointment to the custom house in Boston, was vulnerable to the politics of the spoils system. Hawthorne was a Democrat and lost this job due to the change of administration in Washington after the presidential election of 1848. He wrote a letter of protest to the Boston Daily Advertiser which was attacked by the Whigs and supported by the Democrats, making Hawthorne's dismissal a much-talked about event in New England. He was deeply affected by the death of his mother in late July, calling it "the darkest hour I ever lived". He was appointed the corresponding secretary of the Salem Lyceum in 1848. Guests who came to speak that season included Emerson, Thoreau, Louis Agassiz, and Theodore Parker.

Hawthorne returned to writing and published The Scarlet Letter in mid-March 1850, including a preface that refers to his three-year tenure in the Custom House and makes several allusions to local politicians—who did not appreciate their treatment. It was one of the first mass-produced books in America, selling 2,500 volumes within ten days and earning Hawthorne $1,500 over 14 years. The book was pirated by booksellers in London and became a best-seller in the United States; it initiated his most lucrative period as a writer. Hawthorne's friend Edwin Percy Whipple objected to the novel's "morbid intensity" and its dense psychological details, writing that the book "is therefore apt to become, like Hawthorne, too painfully anatomical in his exhibition of them", though 20th-century writer D. H. Lawrence said that there could be no more perfect work of the American imagination than The Scarlet Letter.

Hawthorne and his family moved to a small red farmhouse near Lenox, Massachusetts, at the end of March 1850. He became friends with Herman Melville beginning on August 5, 1850, when the authors met at a picnic hosted by a mutual friend. Melville had just read Hawthorne's short story collection Mosses from an Old Manse, and his unsigned review of the collection was printed in The Literary World on August 17 and August 24 titled "Hawthorne and His Mosses". Melville wrote that these stories revealed a dark side to Hawthorne, "shrouded in blackness, ten times black". He was composing his novel Moby-Dick at the time, and dedicated the work in 1851 to Hawthorne: "In token of my admiration for his genius, this book is inscribed to Nathaniel Hawthorne."

Hawthorne's time in the Berkshires was very productive. While there, he wrote The House of the Seven Gables (1851), which poet and critic James Russell Lowell said was better than The Scarlet Letter and called "the most valuable contribution to New England history that has been made." He also wrote The Blithedale Romance (1852), his only work written in the first person. He also published A Wonder-Book for Girls and Boys in 1851, a collection of short stories retelling myths which he had been thinking about writing since 1846. Nevertheless, poet Ellery Channing reported that Hawthorne "has suffered much living in this place". The family enjoyed the scenery of the Berkshires, although Hawthorne did not enjoy the winters in their small house. They left on November 21, 1851. Hawthorne noted, "I am sick to death of Berkshire ... I have felt languid and dispirited, during almost my whole residence."

The Wayside and Europe

In May 1852, the Hawthornes returned to Concord where they lived until July 1853. In February, they bought The Hillside, a home previously inhabited by Amos Bronson Alcott and his family, and renamed it The Wayside. Their neighbors in Concord included Emerson and Henry David Thoreau. That year, Hawthorne wrote The Life of Franklin Pierce, the campaign biography of his friend which depicted him as "a man of peaceful pursuits". Horace Mann said, "If he makes out Pierce to be a great man or a brave man, it will be the greatest work of fiction he ever wrote." In the biography, Hawthorne depicts Pierce as a statesman and soldier who had accomplished no great feats because of his need to make "little noise" and so "withdrew into the background". He also left out Pierce's drinking habits, despite rumors of his alcoholism, and emphasized Pierce's belief that slavery could not "be remedied by human contrivances" but would, over time, "vanish like a dream".

With Pierce's election as President, Hawthorne was rewarded in 1853 with the position of United States consul in Liverpool shortly after the publication of Tanglewood Tales. The role was considered the most lucrative foreign service position at the time, described by Hawthorne's wife as "second in dignity to the Embassy in London". His appointment ended in 1857 at the close of the Pierce administration, and the Hawthorne family toured France and Italy. During his time in Italy, the previously clean-shaven Hawthorne grew a bushy mustache.

The family returned to The Wayside in 1860, and that year saw the publication of The Marble Faun, his first new book in seven years. Hawthorne admitted that he had aged considerably, referring to himself as "wrinkled with time and trouble".

Later years and death

At the outset of the American Civil War, Hawthorne traveled with William D. Ticknor to Washington, D.C., where he met Abraham Lincoln and other notable figures. He wrote about his experiences in the essay "Chiefly About War Matters" in 1862.

Failing health prevented him from completing several more romance novels. Hawthorne was suffering from pain in his stomach and insisted on a recuperative trip with his friend Franklin Pierce, though his neighbor Bronson Alcott was concerned that Hawthorne was too ill. While on a tour of the White Mountains, he died in his sleep on May 19, 1864, in Plymouth, New Hampshire. Pierce sent a telegram to Elizabeth Peabody asking her to inform Mrs. Hawthorne in person. Mrs. Hawthorne was too saddened by the news to handle the funeral arrangements herself. Hawthorne's son Julian was a freshman at Harvard College, and he learned of his father's death the next day; coincidentally, he was initiated into the Delta Kappa Epsilon fraternity on the same day by being blindfolded and placed in a coffin.Longfellow wrote a tribute poem to Hawthorne published in 1866 called "The Bells of Lynn". Hawthorne was buried on what is now known as "Authors' Ridge" in Sleepy Hollow Cemetery, Concord, Massachusetts. Pallbearers included Longfellow, Emerson, Alcott, Oliver Wendell Holmes Sr., James Thomas Fields, and Edwin Percy Whipple. Emerson wrote of the funeral: "I thought there was a tragic element in the event, that might be more fully rendered—in the painful solitude of the man, which, I suppose, could no longer be endured, & he died of it."

His wife Sophia and daughter Una were originally buried in England. However, in June 2006, they were reinterred in plots adjacent to Hawthorne.

Writings

Hawthorne had a particularly close relationship with his publishers William Ticknor and James Thomas Fields. Hawthorne once told Fields, "I care more for your good opinion than for that of a host of critics." In fact, it was Fields who convinced Hawthorne to turn The Scarlet Letter into a novel rather than a short story. Ticknor handled many of Hawthorne's personal matters, including the purchase of cigars, overseeing financial accounts, and even purchasing clothes. Ticknor died with Hawthorne at his side in Philadelphia in 1864; according to a friend, Hawthorne was left "apparently dazed".

Literary style and themes

Hawthorne's works belong to romanticism or, more specifically, dark romanticism, cautionary tales that suggest that guilt, sin, and evil are the most inherent natural qualities of humanity. Many of his works are inspired by Puritan New England, combining historical romance loaded with symbolism and deep psychological themes, bordering on surrealism. His depictions of the past are a version of historical fiction used only as a vehicle to express common themes of ancestral sin, guilt and retribution. His later writings also reflect his negative view of the Transcendentalism movement.

Hawthorne was predominantly a short story writer in his early career. Upon publishing Twice-Told Tales, however, he noted, "I do not think much of them," and he expected little response from the public. His four major romances were written between 1850 and 1860: The Scarlet Letter (1850), The House of the Seven Gables (1851), The Blithedale Romance (1852) and The Marble Faun (1860). Another novel-length romance, Fanshawe, was published anonymously in 1828. Hawthorne defined a romance as being radically different from a novel by not being concerned with the possible or probable course of ordinary experience. In the preface to The House of the Seven Gables, Hawthorne describes his romance-writing as using "atmospherical medium as to bring out or mellow the lights and deepen and enrich the shadows of the picture". The picture, Daniel Hoffman found, was one of "the primitive energies of fecundity and creation."

Critics have applied feminist perspectives and historicist approaches to Hawthorne's depictions of women. Feminist scholars are interested particularly in Hester Prynne: they recognize that while she herself could not be the "destined prophetess" of the future, the "angel and apostle of the coming revelation" must nevertheless "be a woman." Camille Paglia saw Hester as mystical, "a wandering goddess still bearing the mark of her Asiatic origins ... moving serenely in the magic circle of her sexual nature". Lauren Berlant termed Hester "the citizen as woman [personifying] love as a quality of the body that contains the purest light of nature," her resulting "traitorous political theory" a "Female Symbolic" literalization of futile Puritan metaphors. Historicists view Hester as a protofeminist and avatar of the self-reliance and responsibility that led to women's suffrage and reproductive emancipation. Anthony Splendora found her literary genealogy among other archetypally fallen but redeemed women, both historic and mythic. As examples, he offers Psyche of ancient legend; Heloise of twelfth-century France's tragedy involving world-renowned philosopher Peter Abelard; Anne Hutchinson (America's first heretic, circa 1636), and Hawthorne family friend Margaret Fuller. In Hester's first appearance, Hawthorne likens her, "infant at her bosom", to Mary, Mother of Jesus, "the image of Divine Maternity". In her study of Victorian literature, in which such "galvanic outcasts" as Hester feature prominently, Nina Auerbach went so far as to name Hester's fall and subsequent redemption, "the novel's one unequivocally religious activity". Regarding Hester as a deity figure, Meredith A. Powers found in Hester's characterization "the earliest in American fiction that the archetypal Goddess appears quite graphically," like a Goddess "not the wife of traditional marriage, permanently subject to a male overlord"; Powers noted "her syncretism, her flexibility, her inherent ability to alter and so avoid the defeat of secondary status in a goal-oriented civilization".

Aside from Hester Prynne, the model women of Hawthorne's other novels—from Ellen Langton of Fanshawe to Zenobia and Priscilla of The Blithedale Romance, Hilda and Miriam of The Marble Faun and Phoebe and Hepzibah of The House of the Seven Gables—are more fully realized than his male characters, who merely orbit them. This observation is equally true of his short-stories, in which central females serve as allegorical figures: Rappaccini's beautiful but life-altering, garden-bound, daughter; almost-perfect Georgiana of "The Birthmark"; the sinned-against (abandoned) Ester of "Ethan Brand"; and goodwife Faith Brown, linchpin of Young Goodman Brown's very belief in God. "My Faith is gone!" Brown exclaims in despair upon seeing his wife at the Witches' Sabbath. Perhaps the most sweeping statement of Hawthorne's impetus comes from Mark Van Doren: "Somewhere, if not in the New England of his time, Hawthorne unearthed the image of a goddess supreme in beauty and power."

Hawthorne also wrote nonfiction. In 2008, the Library of America selected Hawthorne's "A show of wax-figures" for inclusion in its two-century retrospective of American True Crime.

176

Criticism

In "Hawthorne and His Mosses", Herman Melville wrote a passionate argument for Hawthorne to be among the burgeoning American literary canon, "He is one of the new, and far better generation of your writers." In this review of Mosses from an Old Manse, Melville describes an affinity for Hawthorne that would only increase: "I feel that this Hawthorne has dropped germinous seeds into my soul. He expands and deepens down, the more I contemplate him; and further, and further, shoots his strong New-England roots into the hot soil of my Southern soul." Edgar Allan Poe wrote important reviews of both Twice-Told Tales and Mosses from an Old Manse. Poe's assessment was partly informed by his contempt of allegory and moral tales, and his chronic accusations of plagiarism, though he admitted,

> The style of Mr. Hawthorne is purity itself. His tone is singularly effective—wild, plaintive, thoughtful, and in full accordance with his themes ... We look upon him as one of the few men of indisputable genius to whom our country has as yet given birth.

Ralph Waldo Emerson wrote, "Nathaniel Hawthorne's reputation as a writer is a very pleasing fact, because his writing is not good for anything, and this is a tribute to the man." Henry James praised Hawthorne, saying, "The fine thing in Hawthorne is that he cared for the deeper psychology, and that, in his way, he tried to become familiar with it." Poet John Greenleaf Whittier wrote that he admired the "weird and subtle beauty" in Hawthorne's tales. Evert Augustus Duyckinck said of Hawthorne, "Of the American writers destined to live, he is the most original, the one least indebted to foreign models or literary precedents of any kind."

Contemporary response to Hawthorne's work praised his sentimentality and moral purity while more modern evaluations focus on the dark psychological complexity. Beginning in the 1950s, critics have focused on symbolism and didacticism.

The critic Harold Bloom opined that only Henry James and William Faulkner challenge Hawthorne's position as the greatest American novelist, although he admitted that he favored James as the greatest American novelist.

Bloom saw Hawthorne's greatest works to be principally The Scarlet Letter, followed by The Marble Faun and certain short stories, including "My Kinsman, Major Molineux", "Young Goodman Brown", "Wakefield", and "Feathertop". (Source: Wikipedia)

NOTABLE WORKS

NOVELS

Fanshawe (published anonymously, 1828)

The Scarlet Letter (1850)

The House of the Seven Gables (1851)

The Blithedale Romance (1852)

The Marble Faun: Or, The Romance of Monte Beni (1860) (as Transformation: Or, The Romance of Monte Beni, UK publication, same year)

The Dolliver Romance (1863) (unfinished)

Septimius Felton; or, the Elixir of Life (unfinished, published in the Atlantic Monthly, 1872)

Doctor Grimshawe's Secret: A Romance (unfinished, with preface and notes by Julian Hawthorne, 1882)

SHORT STORY COLLECTIONS

Twice-Told Tales (1837)

Grandfather's Chair (1840)

Mosses from an Old Manse (1846)

A Wonder-Book for Girls and Boys (1851)

The Snow-Image, and Other Twice-Told Tales (1852)

Tanglewood Tales (1853)

The Dolliver Romance and Other Pieces (1876)

The Great Stone Face and Other Tales of the White Mountains (1889)

SELECTED SHORT STORIES

"The Hollow of the Three Hills" (1830)

"Roger Malvin's Burial" (1832)

"My Kinsman, Major Molineux" (1832)

"The Minister's Black Veil" (1832)

"Young Goodman Brown" (1835)

"The Gray Champion" (1835)

"The White Old Maid" (1835)

"Wakefield" (1835)

"The Ambitious Guest" (1835)

"The Man of Adamant" (1837)

"The May-Pole of Merry Mount" (1837)

"The Great Carbuncle" (1837)

"Dr. Heidegger's Experiment" (1837)

"A Virtuoso's Collection" (May 1842)

"The Birth-Mark" (March 1843)

"The Celestial Railroad" (1843)

"Egotism; or, The Bosom-Serpent" (1843)

"Earth's Holocaust" (1844)

"Rappaccini's Daughter" (1844)

"P.'s Correspondence" (1845)

"The Artist of the Beautiful" (1846)

"Fire Worship" (1846)

"Ethan Brand" (1850)

"The Great Stone Face" (1850)

"Feathertop" (1852)

NONFICTION

Twenty Days with Julian & Little Bunny (written 1851, published 1904)

Our Old Home (1863)

Passages from the French and Italian Notebooks (1871)

CPSIA information can be obtained
at www.ICGtesting.com
Printed in the USA
LVHW050110140720
660559LV00004B/439

9 789390 170326